W9-BRF-948

"Nothing I have seen provides better spiritual equipment for today's youth to fight and win the spiritual battle raging around them than Bill Myers's Forbidden Doors series. Every Christian family should have the whole set."

C. Peter Wagner
President, Global Harvest Ministries

"During the past 18 years as my husband and I have been involved in youth ministry, we have seen a *definite* need for these books. Bill fills the need with comedy, romance, action, and riveting suspense with clear teaching. It's a nonstop page-turner!"

Robin Jones Gunn
Author, Christy Miller series

"There is a tremendous increase of interest for teens in the occult. Everyone is exploiting and capitalizing on this hunger, but no one is providing answers. Until now. I highly recommend the Forbidden Doors series and encourage any family with teens to purchase it."

James Riordan
Author of authorized biography of
Oliver Stone, and music critic

"Bill Myers's books will help equip families. It's interesting, too, that the Sunday school curriculum market, for which I write, is examining topics such as reincarnation and out-of-body experiences. The Forbidden Doors books are timely."

Carla Williams
Mother and freelance author

"Fast-moving, exciting, and loaded with straight-forward answers to tough questions, Forbidden Doors is Bill Myers at his best."
Jon Henderson
Author

The Forbidden Doors Series

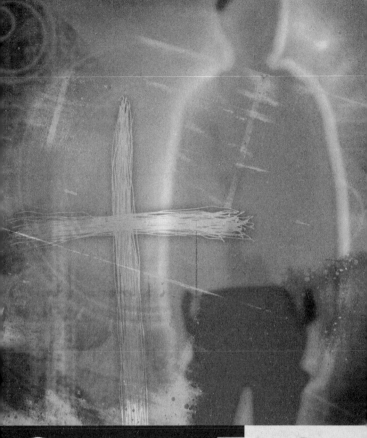

FORBIDDEN ● DOORS

the encounter

BILL MYERS

Tyndale House Publishers, Inc.   Wheaton, Illinois

Visit the exciting Web site for kids at www.cool2read.com
and the Forbidden Doors Web site at
www.forbiddendoors.com

Designed by Julie Chen

Published in association with the literary agency of Alive
Communications, Inc., 7680 Goddard Street, Suite 200,
Colorado Springs, CO 80920.

ISBN 0-8423-5738-6, mass paper

Printed in the United States of America

08 07 06 05 04 03 02
7   6   5   4   3   2   1

*To Carla Williams
and family, for
your encouragement
and help.*

This evil man will come to do the work of Satan with counterfeit power and signs and miracles. He will use every kind of wicked deception to fool those who are on their way to destruction because they refuse to believe the truth that would save them.

2 Thessalonians 2:9-10

1

ow are you coming?" Philip asked as he peered over the stack of library books at Krissi.

The girl sighed and lifted her perfectly manicured nails to brush her perfect dark hair out of her perfect green eyes. "If you keep interrupting my concentration," she complained, "nothing will happen."

"Sorry," he said.

"Xandrak only writes through me if I relax and keep my mind clear."

Philip chuckled and returned to his books. If there was ever a person who would be able to keep her mind clear, it was Krissi. As far as he knew she hadn't had a deep thought in years. But getting her to relax was another thing. Let's face it—opening yourself up to the influence of aliens and allowing them to write messages through you would tend to make anyone a little nervous.

But that's what Krissi was doing, and she was getting good at it. Very good. The process was called automatic handwriting, and during the past week its effects had grown stronger than ever. Often the writing would repeat the same phrases over and over again. Phrases that always emphasized Krissi was a specially chosen Light Worker, that she would help usher in the New Age of spiritual enlightenment, and that if she listened carefully to the Ascended Masters, she could help cleanse the planet and rescue it from its self-destruction.

Of course, neither Philip nor Krissi was sure what all of this stuff meant, but what they did understand sounded pretty cool.

Krissi also had been warned, over and over, to stay away from people with "dark emotions"—especially narrow-minded Christians like Rebecca Williams, Becka's boyfriend, Ryan, and now Julie Mitchell. It made no difference that they all used to be friends. Their old-fashioned way of thinking, their "clinging to outdated religion," could pose a real threat.

At least, that's what the messages kept saying.

They said one other thing, too—and this was the phrase that had Krissi the most excited. They told her she would be "making contact with an intergalactic race." Soon.

That's why Krissi was so busy trying to connect with Xandrak, her alien guide. And that's why Philip was poring through every book on UFOs that he could find in the public library. If there was even the slightest chance of actually meeting inhabitants from another world, he wanted to be prepared.

At first Philip didn't buy into all of this UFO nonsense. As an intellectual type, he believed everything had to be proven. Sure, he knew Krissi's automatic writing was legitimate—they'd tested it a dozen times. Not only was the handwriting entirely different from her own, but whatever or whoever was moving her hand knew things Krissi couldn't possibly know.

Still, to believe it was actually somebody from another planet, to believe that an extraterrestrial was actually writing through his girlfriend, well, that was a bit much for Philip. But as the information in her writing continued to line up with his research, Philip was finding it harder and harder to deny what Krissi was telling him.

"Check it out," he said, referring to the book in front of him. "It says here that one out of ten adults in the United States has seen a UFO."

"No kidding?" she asked.

He nodded. "And not just crackpots. It says here that the pharaohs of Egypt saw them, as well as Christopher Columbus, Andrew Jackson, NASA astronauts."

Krissi nodded and repositioned the pencil on her writing pad so it would flow more smoothly. Still, nothing happened.

Philip continued. "Ninety-five percent of the sightings can be explained, but there's still 5 percent that no one has an answer for. Oh, and listen to this: 'Currently there are over one thousand documented cases of personal contact with alien creatures.'"

"You mean where people actually meet them?"

"Uh-huh. It also says there are UFO channelers and automatic handwriters around the world."

Krissi's excitement drooped. "So there's

more people than just me doing this type of writing?"

"Yeah, tons. In fact, it says—"

"Philip," she interrupted. "Look at my hand. It's starting!"

They both looked down at the paper as her hand began to write letters. It was the same handwriting they'd seen before.

"This is so cool," she chirped. "I'm not having to zone out or daydream or anything. Now it's just happening as I sit here talking."

Philip cocked his head to watch the letters form. "I guess that means it's getting stronger."

"He," Krissi corrected. *"He's* getting stronger."

Philip shrugged. He still wasn't entirely convinced.

They continued watching, but instead of the New Age ramblings that Krissi's hand usually wrote, this message was short and to the point:

GREETINGS IN THE NAME OF THE INTERGALACTIC ALLIANCE. THE TIME FOR OUR RENDEZVOUS HAS ARRIVED. PREPARE FOR ENCOUNTER AT OLD LOGGING ROAD OFF HIGHWAY 72, NORTH OF SETH CREEK. 8:00 P.M. PEACE.

XANDRAK

The pencil came to a stop. Philip's and Krissi's hearts pounded as they stared at the message. Neither fully believed what they saw. Finally, Philip looked at his watch. "It's 7:07. . . ."

Krissi nodded, swallowing back a wave of both fear and excitement. "If we're going to meet him we better hurry."

~

"Sweetheart, I'm just a little concerned, that's all."

"Everything's fine, Mom."

"But you're spending all your evenings there. And Becka and I, we hardly ever see you anymore."

Scott could feel his mother closing in. If he didn't hurry and ease her fears, she could stop him from going over to Hubert's at all. He reached across the dinner table for the casserole dish and piled up an extra portion of Hamburger Whatever onto his plate. Eating was a good way to stall while he thought of the best approach. Come to think of it, eating was good for just about anything these days. At fifteen, Scott Williams was growing faster than a weed, and food was one thing he could never get enough of.

Food and playing Crypts and Wizards.

The game had been going on for about

two weeks now. Darryl, his best friend, had invited him over to his cousin Hubert's house. As a part-time computer whiz and full-time weirded-out genius, Hubert had modified an incredible fantasy role-playing game. Each night, he would lock himself away in an upstairs bedroom and run the master computer while Scott and a half dozen other players plugged in their own computers downstairs and tried to track down the treasure Hubert had hidden in a special crypt—a crypt that only he had the map for.

The game was incredible. Not only did it give Scott a chance to really use his mind, but he could put that incredible imagination of his to work as well. Each of the players played a character with special strengths, personalities, and magical powers. Some were elves, others werewolves, warriors, warlocks, wizards, zombies, and the list went on. You could be anything you wanted. And nothing matched the excitement of battling as a supernatural character who had special weapons, spells, and magical powers.

Of course, Scott knew some of this stuff could be pretty dark at times, and it did make him just a little bit nervous. But, hey, it was only a game. Just make-believe. All in his imagination.

The character he had created for himself— a mystical holy man by the name of Ttocs (Scott spelled backward)—had many of the same personality traits he did: a strong sense of justice, a belief in the supernatural, and a love for people. As the game continued over the hours, the days, and on into the weeks, Scott had grown more and more attached to the little guy. Together the two fought off the ghouls and monsters that Hubert—and other players' characters— threw at them. All this while carefully planning their route to get to the treasure.

"Scotty, are you sure it's really that healthy?" Becka asked from across the table.

"What's that supposed to mean?" Scott didn't exactly snap at his older sister, but he wasn't smiling, either. What business was it of hers? Sure, the two of them were extra close. There was something about growing up in the Brazilian rain forest and only having each other as playmates that created a bit of a bond. Then there was losing Dad in the airplane crash less than a year ago. And, of course, all that occult stuff they'd gone through since they moved to the States. Still, that didn't give her the right to meddle.

Becka shrugged. "It just seems like spending all your time doing something like that isn't so smart."

Scott tried to hide his irritation. "Relax.

I'm just honing my computer skills. Besides, I'm getting a chance to exercise my imagination and—" he threw her a pointed look— "make a few friends along the way."

Becka glanced down.

He'd hit his mark. It was a little mean, but he'd had to find some way of telling her to back off. He knew Becka had a hard time making friends; on the self-image scale of 1 to 10 she was about a –3. He also knew that Philip and Krissi, two of the few friends she did have, had just cut her off.

Becka grew silent. He knew she'd caught his drift. Now there was only Mom to worry about.

"Well—" his mother wiped her mouth and rose from her chair to get dessert—"I'm not saying no. Yet."

Scott relaxed.

"But," she continued, "I want you to give the matter some serious thought."

Scott nodded, grateful the inquisition had come to an end. He snuck a peek at his watch. 7:45. He had to hurry. The game would be resuming in fifteen minutes, and he couldn't miss a second of it.

～

The Jeep Wrangler raced down Highway 72 with the CD blasting an old Doors tune. It wasn't Philip's favorite music, but since his car was in the shop and the Wrangler was borrowed from Dad, he had to listen to whatever tunes Dad had. The moon was full and shrouded with only a thin layer of fog coming in from the coast. There was plenty of light to see the logging road . . . if they only knew where it was.

He glanced at the dashboard clock. 8:10. They were already late—thanks to Krissi's insistence that they stop by her house so she could change. Let's face it, the last thing in the world you want to do when meeting aliens from another planet is to be seen wearing a sweatshirt that's three months out of fashion. Not when you have a new silk vest and capris to wear. Philip sighed and pressed down on the accelerator.

He loved Krissi. Everybody knew it. They didn't understand it, but they knew it. It seemed so odd that Philip, with his super-intellect, would show the slightest interest in Krissi, with her superairheadedness. Maybe it had something to do with her impulsive way of life. Philip had to think everything through five times before he even considered doing it; Krissi just up and did. When this approach didn't make him crazy, Philip loved the excitement and freedom it brought.

But his feelings went far deeper than that.

Maybe it had to do with growing up next door to her and being best friends all their lives. Or maybe it had to do with Philip's mom taking his two sisters and deserting him and his dad without a word. Krissi had been the only one there for him. Feeling for him. Aching with him. Holding him for hours one afternoon when he couldn't stop crying.

Whatever the reason for their love, if the phrase "opposites attract" had ever applied to a couple, it applied to them. Krissi was Philip's breath of freedom and fresh air; he was her rock and reality check.

"We must have passed it," Krissi shouted over the music. "Turn around."

Philip threw her a look. "Did you see anything?"

She shook her head. "No, but we passed it. I know we did."

"Krissi . . ."

"Don't ask me how I know, I just—I just know it. I feel it, OK?"

Philip gave her another look.

"We haven't got much time," she insisted. "Please, trust me on this."

He glanced at the clock. 8:11. They were going to be late anyway, and if Krissi was so sure . . .

He slowed the Wrangler, pulled to the

side, and threw the vehicle into a sharp U-turn. The gravel sprayed as he gunned the engine and slid back onto the road going the opposite direction. Once again he looked at Krissi. She was concentrating, staring out her window.

There were no other cars in sight. Philip clicked on the high beams and picked up speed. Ever since their little supernatural encounter at the Hawthorne mansion, Krissi's automatic handwriting wasn't the only thing that had grown stronger. Her intuition, her ability to sense things she didn't know, had increased. She could perceive things others didn't.

Philip smiled. Of course, some of this was just her natural spontaneity, like the time she'd felt "impressed" to take the day off and go to the beach instead of taking a geometry midterm. Or the time she felt "directed" to order silver-plated hunting knives on the shopping channel. He shook his head slightly. She'd never hunted in her life and didn't know anyone who did. But that was all some time ago. Lately . . . Philip glanced at her. Lately Krissi's insights tended to be right on the money.

"There!" she shouted. "Right there!"

Philip looked just in time to see a secluded opening whisk by. He hit the brakes, threw the Jeep into reverse, and quickly backed up. Sure enough, there it was. With all the underbrush, it had been practically invisible. But now you could clearly see it was the remains of an old logging road.

"It looks pretty overgrown in there," Krissi said.

Philip grinned at her and reached down. "That's why we've got four-wheel drive, kiddo." He pulled a smaller gearshift forward, turned the Jeep toward the opening, and they began bouncing and jostling up the remains of the old dirt road.

Bushes scraped the sides of the vehicle and an occasional tree branch slapped at the windshield. Philip took it slow in case there were also rocks or ruts hiding, waiting to rip out his oil pan.

"What do you think we'll see?" he asked. "Flying saucers? Little green men?"

Krissi craned her neck to look up into the sky. "I'm not sure." The fog had grown thicker, allowing only the most determined stars to burn through. She turned and looked out her window at the passing brush and trees. "Xandrak wouldn't tell us to show up here if it wasn't something . . . hold it! What was that?"

"What?"

"Stop the car!"

Philip hit the brakes. He reached over to turn off the CD. Now there was just the quiet idling of the motor.

Krissi looked over her shoulder through the window of the backseat. "It looked like . . ." She hesitated.

"Like what?"

"A cow."

Philip chuckled. "Krissi, there aren't any cows around here. The nearest ranch is twenty miles away."

"It was a cow, I'm sure of it. It had four legs, horns, everything." She reached for the door and opened it.

"Krissi, don't—" But he was too late. The door was already open and she was stepping out. Philip sighed and followed suit, uncoiling his six-foot frame from behind the wheel.

Once outside, he talked to her over the roof as she walked away. "Even if it is a cow, that's not exactly what we're looking for."

~

"I know." Krissi delicately pushed aside a branch that threatened to mess her hair or, worse yet, soil her vest. "But doesn't it, like, surprise you that a cow would be way out here in the middle of the woods?"

He gave no answer.

"Philip?"

Still no response.

"Philip, answer me." She turned back to the car and saw there was a good reason for his silence.

Philip was staring at a diamond-shaped object that hovered a hundred feet above them in the sky.

Krissi moved for a better look. It wasn't just one diamond-shaped object, but three. Three craft hovering in a perfect triangular formation. They were absolutely silent, but they pulsed various colors—first red, then green, then yellow, then back to red.

She watched as Philip continued to stare for another half minute. Even then he never took his eyes off the objects. "OK," he said hoarsely. "Now what? . . ."

2

As if answering his question, the formation of lights started moving forward.

"They're going!" Philip cried. "They didn't see us. Hey!" he shouted. "Hey, we're down here!" He waved his arms. "We're down here. Hey! We're—"

"They know," Krissi said quietly. Her voice

was so calm he turned to look at her. She stood on the other side of the Jeep. "They want us to follow."

"They what?"

"They want us to follow them. They're staying above the road so we can follow."

Philip stared at her, then looked back to the moving objects. Sure enough, they were moving forward, but very slowly and directly over the road that stretched before them.

He climbed back into the Jeep. Krissi slid into the passenger seat. He started to put the vehicle into gear, then turned and asked, "You sure we want to do this?"

Krissi smiled. "What do you think?"

Philip had no choice. He wished he had, but the time to chicken out would have been back at the library or at Krissi's house or on the highway. Not here, not now. He nodded, dropped the Jeep into gear, and they started forward.

Krissi's eyes stayed glued to the windshield, focused on the pulsing lights that led them. They never grew brighter, they never grew dimmer. They just continued the same pulse from red to green to yellow and back to red.

As Philip drove he felt a chill start somewhere in his gut and slowly work its way up his back and into his shoulders. It was uncanny, the way the lights stayed in perfect formation, the way they kept the same distance from them, slowing when he had to slow, speeding up when he sped up.

The only sound was the jarring and bouncing of the Jeep as it dipped in and out of the holes and ruts. Neither Philip nor Krissi spoke. They remained as silent as the lights.

The road finally opened onto a large grassy area half the size of a football field. The lights slowly veered from the road and crossed to the far left side of the field, near a stand of pine trees. There they came to a stop and waited.

Philip hesitated. He was not about to get out of the vehicle and follow the hovering craft. Nor was he crazy about turning off the road and traveling through some unknown field at night. Who knew what ditches, stumps, or drop-offs lay ahead. Still, what other choice did he have? Reluctantly, he eased the Jeep off the road and crept through the field. It took several minutes, but at last he pulled to a stop twenty or so feet from the lights.

"Krissi?"

"Shh . . ." She was still staring up through the windshield.

Philip looked at her. Was she sensing something? Was she hearing something? He glanced back up to the silent lights.

Suddenly the Jeep's engine began to sputter. Then cough. Then it quit altogether. Philip glanced at the gas gauge. There was still a quarter tank left. Then he realized it wasn't just the motor that had stopped. The headlights were gone, too.

He reached over to the key, switched it off, then back on. The engine turned but would not start. He turned the ignition off, then tried again. Same result.

"Don't worry about it," Krissi said.

"What?"

"It's OK."

He looked at her, not understanding. He gave the ignition a third try, this time grinding the starter over and over again.

Suddenly, there was a blast of light—so bright and intense that he thought the craft above him had blown up. But it wasn't an explosion; it was a light beam, five feet in diameter and as bright as the sun. It slowly extended from the center of the three crafts toward the stand of pine trees.

Philip and Krissi shielded their eyes as the light continued to stretch toward the trees, but when it hit the top branches, it did not illuminate them. It ignited them. Instantly. They exploded into a giant fireball.

Krissi screamed as they covered their faces from the light and heat that blasted through the windshield.

Philip fumbled for the ignition. He had to get them out of there! He turned the key. Nothing.

He looked back at the beam of light and froze. It was moving—so slowly that at first he thought it was the hot wavy air from the fire playing tricks, like a mirage. But this was no trick. The beam was moving off the blazing trees and inching its way toward them, igniting everything in its path.

"Philip, get us out of here!"

Philip pumped the accelerator. Still nothing.

The light continued toward them.

"Philip!"

"I'm trying!" he shouted. *"I'm trying!"*

Now the beam was fifteen feet away. . . .

"PHILIP!!"

His hand was shaking. It was so sweaty that the key slipped as he tried to turn it.

Twelve feet, ten . . .

Now they could hear the moisture from the grass and shrubs hissing and sizzling under the approaching heat. Pieces of wood cracked and popped as if in a fireplace.

Eight feet . . .

"Philip!"

Five . . .

He reached for his door. "Let's get out of here!"

21

"What?"

"Run! Get out of the car! *Run!*"

Then, as instantly as it had started, the beam stopped. There was no light. Only the blazing trees ahead of them and the burning undergrowth beside them. Philip stared. The fire would not spread. He knew that. Everything was too damp and wet. He leaned against the wheel, trying to catch his breath, trying to steady himself.

Krissi sat beside him, shaking like a leaf.

They sat in the car, unable to move, as the pines continued burning. Both followed the line of charred vegetation, cut with razorlike accuracy from the trees to within five feet of their Jeep.

Philip turned to Krissi. The light from the fire danced and played across her frightened face. With one hand he wiped away the sweat that had fallen into his eyes. With the other he reached out to her. "You OK?"

She nodded.

He craned his neck to look back up through the windshield.

When Krissi finally spoke, her voice was weak and thin. "Are . . . are they still there?"

The light from the fire was so bright it was impossible to see anything in the sky.

"It's too bright," he said. "I can't tell." He heard the handle to the passenger door turn.

His eyes shot to Krissi, who was opening the door and getting out. "Where you going?!"

"I can't stay in here. I've got to go."

"Krissi, we're safe in here. At least safer than—"

But Krissi would not listen. "I can't stay in here!" She stepped down into the knee-high grass. She tilted her head up toward the sky. Whatever expression she had on her face suddenly froze. "Philip . . ." Her voice was high and faraway.

"What? What is it?"

"Philip . . . they're coming. . . ."

"Krissi, get back insi—"

The car pitched violently to the right.

"Philip!"

With the jolt came another light. Glaring. Powerful. Overcoming every shadow, every inch of darkness. But this light was different from the first. It was blue and carried no heat. Only power. The vehicle heaved under another impact and began to rock.

"Philip!!"

When he spotted her, she was still outside but clinging to the door with all of her might. Her feet were parallel to the ground and rising. Something was sucking her upward!

"Philip!" she screamed, terrified.

He lunged for her, but the shaking of the

car tossed him like a pinball. One minute he'd grabbed her arm through the open window, the next he was thrown to the floorboard.

Krissi's grip on the door had been broken. She was now clinging to the side mirror, screaming hysterically. Philip struggled back up into the seat. He reached out the window and grabbed her wrists—both of them. They were so slick with sweat that he could barely hang on. He could no longer see her legs. They were above her head as she clung to the door, screaming.

"Don't let me go! Don't let me go!"

The car continued to lunge back and forth. For a brief second their eyes connected. There was no mistaking Krissi's helpless horror. Adrenaline surged through Philip. He would save her. He would not let go of her, not at any cost. Still clinging to her wrists, he pulled himself to her window. But his grip was slipping.

"Hang on!" he shouted. "Hang on!"

"I can't! Philip, help m—"

The car lurched violently. Krissi screamed as her hands slipped away from the mirror. The pull was too great. Philip could no longer hold her. She slid from his grip and disappeared into the night.

"Krissi! *Krissi!!*"

Becka bolted awake in her room. She'd gone to bed early and had barely dropped off when she had a dream. But this wasn't just your run-of-the-mill dream. It was another one of those dreams. She couldn't remember any specifics. Just terror.

And Krissi. Somehow she knew the terror involved Krissi.

For days Becka had tried to warn her one-time friend about playing with the automatic handwriting. Becka knew the experience was legitimate. She knew somebody or something was moving Krissi's hand.

She also knew that the somebody or something was evil.

Becka, Ryan, even her other friend, Julie, had all tried to warn Krissi. But the auto-writing messages had said the three of them were not to be trusted. So Krissi cut them off. It had been painful for Becka, but it was far from the first time she had been snubbed because of her faith.

Actually, it went further than just her faith. Over the past several months Becka had been developing a certain skill, a "calling" if you will. It wasn't something she wanted. On the contrary, what she really wanted was to blend into the crowd and be like everyone else. But that didn't seem to be her lot.

Instead, with all the supernatural battles she'd been involved in, she had developed a reputation as someone who was all too familiar with the occult. Someone who knew what to look out for, and if necessary, someone who could battle it.

Kids at school had started calling her the All-School Ghostbuster.

Now, as she lay in the darkness of her room, she could feel her gift at work again. The old, familiar dread surrounded her—but it wasn't dread for herself. It was dread for Krissi.

Prayer wasn't something Becka was great at. Truth was, she knew she should be doing a lot more of it than she did. But with schoolwork, friends, TV, and the fast-paced life of high school, it was usually pretty hard to find time. Still, she tried.

Especially tonight. She had to. When she felt this kind of dread, she knew she had no option. It was the only way she could battle . . . whatever was going on. And, at least for tonight, it was the only thing she could do for Krissi, the only way she could help.

So Becka started to pray.

*

Scott stared intently at the computer screen. Ttocs, the mystical holy man he had created, was locked in mortal combat with a blood-drinking banshee. According to Hubert, the Crypt Master, the ghoul had been lying in wait for just such an attack. Now the monster leaped onto Ttocs's neck, dug her fangs into his arteries, and sucked with all her might. Not only was she drawing Ttocs's blood, but his brains were also being sucked through the hollow, needlelike fangs.

Scott hit the Alt, Shift, and R keys on his keyboard and watched numbers flash across his screen. This was the computer's version of throwing dice.

The numbers appeared: 11, 4, and 3. Scott groaned. The 11 meant he got away, but not without losing most of his mental abilities. The two low numbers meant he had lost his armor and long sword. In short, Ttocs had survived. Barely.

Scott thumped his desk in frustration.

Darryl, who was sitting in the station beside him, gave a loud sniff. "So, it's just a game, huh?" He grinned.

Scott ignored him. "What good is it being a holy man when there's goons like that who can destroy you in one round?"

"You shouldn't have used your sword."

"What do you mean?"

"You're a mystic, right? A holy man?"

"So . . ."

"So, use your telekinesis powers—your magic. Instead of fighting them with swords, use your spells."

Suddenly Scott's screen began to flash. One of the other players was challenging him to combat. He'd obviously smelled blood and was close enough to go in for the kill.

Again Scott rolled the dice. Again the numbers were too low. And thanks to the attack of a common, everyday flesh eater, the great Ttocs suddenly died. His internal organs had been devoured and the rest of his brain sucked out. Scott slapped the desk again. He was out of the game.

"And another thing," Darryl sniffed while pushing up his glasses, "you were only playing halfway."

"What do you mean?"

"To really win at this thing, you have to play body, mind, and soul."

"I was."

"No way. Your character was too nice. Next time make up somebody ruthless and blood-thirsty. Save the nice-guy act for reality."

Scott gave him a look, then turned back to his screen and watched as his name and location were bleeped from the map. His face flushed with anger. He knew it was only a game, but still . . . part of him had been up on that screen. Part of him had just been destroyed.

He folded his arms and leaned back. *So Darryl thinks I'm holding back, does he? That I was too nice? OK, fine. Next time I'll create a better character. Next time I'll play with everything I have. They want bloodthirsty and ruthless, they'll get bloodthirsty and ruthless.* He smiled grimly. *The new and improved Ttocs will be unstoppable.*

As he waited for Darryl and the others to finish for the evening, Scott grabbed a paper and pencil, rose to his feet, and crossed to the Game Book on the center table. This was a book that listed various types of characters, explaining their abilities, weapons, powers, personalities, and so forth. He flipped the book open. He would need all the help and hints he could get. He would still keep the name Ttocs. But this new version would be the best player they had ever seen.

3

Krissi!"

Philip threw open the car door and staggered into the blinding blue light. She was his life, his reason for living. If she had to meet some awful fate, he would meet it with her. If he had to give up his life to save hers, he would.

But once he stepped outside, the light was no longer blue. It was orangish white, like the sun. And it no longer hovered above him. It was rising over the mountains in the east, right where the sun would rise.

Philip shook his head and blinked. It *was* the sun. He was staring at the rising sun!

He rubbed his eyes and took half a step back. But instead of grass under his feet, he heard the crunch of gravel. His mouth opened in surprise as he saw he was no longer standing in grass, but on asphalt.

What was going on?

He looked around. He wasn't in the field anymore. He was standing next to his dad's Jeep on Highway 72!

"What are you doing out there?"

He spun around to see Krissi sitting up in the passenger's seat. Her eyes were puffy from sleep, but other than that she looked perfectly fine.

"What . . . ?" He swallowed. "Are you OK?"

She gave a long stretch. "Yeah."

He looked back into the sky. It was blue and gorgeous and clear. Not a flying saucer in sight.

"Why didn't you wake me?" she asked. "What time is it?" Before he could check his watch, she squinted at the dash clock. "6:25! My folks are going to kill me. Hurry up, we have to get home."

Philip nodded numbly and crossed to his

side of the Jeep. As he climbed inside, Krissi scolded him again. "You should have woke me."

He reached for the ignition. "I, uh, I didn't know you were asleep."

"Yeah, right," she scoffed. She pulled down the vanity mirror to check her hair and makeup. "I must have really zonked out."

Philip fired up the Jeep. It started on the first try. "What, uh, what was the last thing you remember? Last night, I mean."

She scowled, trying to think. "I was getting out to look for that stupid cow."

Philip took a deep breath to steady himself. "You don't remember seeing those lights? You don't remember getting sucked into the air?"

Krissi gave him a look. "What's that supposed to mean?"

He could find no answer.

"I remember getting out of the car and you telling me I couldn't possibly have seen a cow. You said the nearest ranch was twenty miles away and that—hey, wait a minute."

Philip turned to her.

Krissi was looking into the vanity mirror. "Did you brush my hair?"

"Did I what?"

"My hair, when I was asleep, did you, like, try to brush it or something?"

"Why would I—"

"I never part it on the left."

"What?"

"My hair. That's my worst side. I never part it on the left."

Philip stared. She was right. In all the years he had known her, he had never seen her hair parted on the left. He'd seen it up, he'd seen it back, he'd seen it cropped . . . but he had never seen it parted on the left.

Krissi turned back to him, puzzled, her voice sounding more and more uneasy. "Philip, what's going on?"

~

"Just talk to her, that's all I'm asking."

"Philip," Becka sighed, "she doesn't want to talk to me. She doesn't even want to see me."

"I know . . . but if I can arrange something, if I can get the two of you together?"

Philip stayed glued to her side as Becka arrived at her locker and opened it. The last thing in the world she wanted was another encounter with Krissi. The screaming bout in the hall last week had been enough. The girl was always so dramatic. Normally that didn't bother Becka, but the fact that Krissi's dramatics had been directed at her and that they'd been loud enough for everyone to hear did bother her. A lot.

"Please, just a word," Philip persisted.

"She thinks I'm the enemy," Becka answered. "You know that. She says I'm holding you guys back from evolving to your next spiritual level, whatever *that* means." Becka dumped her books into her locker and grabbed her lunch.

"I think it means we're in way over our heads."

Becka turned to him. "Something happened?"

Philip nodded and looked away. "Last night."

Becka waited, remembering her dreams, remembering her prayers.

"We were supposed to have a meeting with that alien thing, that Xandrak guy."

Becka closed her locker slowly. Philip, the intellectual—Philip, the always confident, always perfect Ken to Krissi's perfect Barbie—was looking very pale. And scared.

"Are you OK?"

He tried to smile, but with little success.

"What happened?"

He cleared his throat and glanced at the floor. But before he could answer, another voice called out.

"Philip?"

They turned to see Krissi standing there, her hands on her hips.

"Hey, Krissi. I, uh, I was just talking to Becka."

She took a step closer. The two girls nodded to each other. Becka could already feel the hall temperature drop several degrees.

Philip continued, trying just a little too hard. "I was telling her about what happened last night, at least what I thought happened, and, uh, she wanted to go out and visit the place. You know, see for herself."

Becka threw him a look, but his eyes did not meet hers.

Krissi turned from one to the other. Finally she shrugged. "I suppose." Then, zeroing in on Becka, she continued, "I mean if it's going to help convince you that it's really happening."

Becka opened her mouth. She was about to explain that she had no doubts something was happening, but Philip stepped in. "That's right, I think it would really help convince her that it's for real."

"Oh, it's real," Krissi repeated. "I called up the Ascension Lady, and she said it was a classic case of alien abduction."

"Of what?" Becka asked.

"You wouldn't understand. But the Ascension Lady does, and she's going to explain it all to us tomorrow."

The Ascension Lady was the woman who owned the New Age bookshop in town and who dabbled in the occult. At one point, up at the Hawthorne mansion, Becka had actually helped her, saving her from a ruthless demonic attack. But it hadn't taken long for the woman to return to her old ways. When Becka found out she'd gone back to the occult, she'd felt a type of defeat—with plenty of pain and regret.

She suspected that was why Krissi was bringing up the Ascension Lady's name—to rub a little more salt in the wound.

"Good." Philip jumped in a little too quickly. "Then we'll meet after school, OK?"

"Whatever." Krissi moved away. "Just as long as she doesn't try any of her hocus-pocus junk. Are you coming?"

"Yeah." Philip turned. Continuing to avoid Becka's gaze, he quickly moved to join Krissi as she entered the moving swarm of students heading for the cafeteria. At the last second he turned and called over his shoulder, "Tell Ryan we'll meet him in the parking lot right after school."

Before Becka could respond he turned and continued down the hall. She stood a long moment, silent and thoughtful.

She didn't like what was happening. Not one bit. But if Krissi and Philip needed her special type of help, did she really have any other choice?

The books had cost Scott nearly fifty bucks—a month's worth of lawn mowing and handyman jobs—but they were worth every penny. He'd gone downtown at lunch to pick them up from the local comic-book store. The first was simply a rule book: *An Encyclopedia for Crypts and Wizards*. But the second book, that was what really held his interest. It was a careful, step-by-step description with charts and diagrams explaining how to create the very best characters for the game.

Scott had started reading it on the way back to school, and thanks to the book's size (small enough to fit behind his geometry text), he continued reading and studying it well into fourth period. Carefully, he went through page after page, jotting down notes on armor, weapons, kill abilities, sexual bent, ruthlessness, passion, using curses, casting spells, speaking with the dead, calling up plagues, divining animal entrails . . . and the list went on.

Of course, he knew these weren't characteristics you'd necessarily want in real life, but, hey, it was just make-believe. Truth is, it was a rush being someone he could never be, doing things he could never do. In fact, when it came right down to it, fantasizing he was Ttocs had been the high point of the last few weeks.

At the moment he was deeply involved in the "Vengeful Characteristics"—when and how to be vengeful, why it can benefit you during a specific round. It was so fascinating that he hadn't even heard Mr. Patton call on him.

"Mr. Williams?" the stocky, bald man repeated. "Mr. Williams?!"

Scott looked up, startled.

"I trust you're not too bored with our discussion."

Still coming out of the daze, Scott answered, "Yes, sir."

The class chuckled.

"What?"

"I mean, no, sir. I mean, yes, sir, I'm not too bored."

"Good. Then do try to stay with us. Given your performance on last week's quiz, I think you'll find the investment well worth the effort."

"Yes, sir," Scott said, feeling his ears start to redden.

Mr. Patton returned to the theorem on the board, and Scott was grateful everyone redirected their attention to the front.

Everyone but Bonnie Eagleman.

Bonnie sat one row up and to the right. In the past she'd made every effort to let Scott know she was interested in him. And, though flattered, Scott had made every effort to avoid her. She was a good kid, just not his type. Now he felt her eyes on him, and she was probably grinning away with those braces.

It was irritating, and Scott was in no mood to deal with it. He'd just been chewed out by Patton and—after spending twenty minutes immersed in vengefulness—he realized he didn't have to put up with it. Ttocs certainly wouldn't.

"Hey," he whispered, motioning for her to come a little closer.

She obeyed, her heart obviously atwitter.

"I've got a question."

She waited eagerly.

"With all that metal in your mouth, when you sleep, does your head, like, point north?"

Bonnie's smile twitched slightly, then faded. The student in front snickered as Bonnie's cheeks turned crimson red and she looked back to the front.

It was one of Scott's better jabs, but he instantly regretted it. He'd hurt her feelings. Actually, destroyed them was more like it. He hadn't meant to be cruel. He just wasn't thinking. OK, OK, he *was* thinking, but more like Ttocs than Scott. He frowned, trying to fight off the guilt and uneasiness.

What had happened? Being cruel wasn't his style. Not at all.

But it *was* Ttocs's style.

~

"So you think this stuff's, like, demonic?" Ryan asked.

Becka took in a deep breath and slowly let it out. The two were riding in Ryan's vintage Mustang and following Philip's Jeep up Highway 72.

"I don't know," she finally said. "You can't say everything is from the devil just because you don't understand it. That's stupid. I don't understand electricity, but that doesn't make it demonic."

Ryan nodded. "Even so, after all the stuff we've been through . . . at the mansion, that so-called angel in Julie's room, Krissi's automatic writing . . . and now whatever Philip claimed he saw . . ."

Becka closed her eyes. Why did she always end up here, involved in something she didn't like? Pulled into the world of the supernatural?

She felt Ryan's hand take hers, and she looked at him. Emotions washed over her.

She admired him so much—his honesty, his
sensitivity . . . and, of course, his looks didn't
hurt, either. Especially the way that thick
black hair constantly fell into those gorgeous
blue eyes.

He'd only been a Christian for a few
weeks, but he'd been exposed to more spiritual warfare than most would have to face in
a lifetime.

The thought didn't exactly thrill her.

"I'm sorry," she said quietly.

"For what?"

"For you always being pulled into this sort
of stuff."

Not missing a beat, he flashed her his
killer grin. "Seems a small price to pay for
the company I get to keep."

Becka couldn't help but smile. Once again
that wonderful warmth spread through her
body. What was with this guy? Couldn't he
see that she was just your basic nobody with
your basic nobody figure and looks? And let's
not forget that wonderful nobody hair . . .
thin, mousy brown, and unable to hold a
style for more than thirty seconds.

He squeezed her hand. She gratefully
returned it. Apparently she was a somebody
to him.

Up ahead, the Jeep slowed and pulled off
the road.

"Looks like we're here," Ryan said as he pulled in behind it.

The two climbed out of the Mustang and walked up to Philip and Krissi.

"It's pretty overgrown in there," Philip said, motioning to the brush-covered logging road.

"How far is it?" Ryan asked.

"'Bout half a mile. Hop in and we'll four-wheel it."

Ryan and Becka climbed into the backseat. "What happened to your convertible?" Ryan asked.

"It's in the shop," Philip said. "My dad's letting me borrow this."

"Cool."

Philip dropped the Jeep into four-wheel drive, and they started the tooth-rattling, bone-jarring journey up the road.

Before too much silence could fill the car, Ryan asked, "It's still a little unclear to me. What exactly is it you two saw?"

"Philip saw it," Krissi corrected. "Not me."

"But . . . you were with him, right?"

Krissi nodded. She looked straight ahead, searching the road. "I just don't remember. The Ascension Lady says with that type of memory lapse, I'm probably repressing some-thing."

"I'm sorry, what?"

43

Philip explained, "There are about ten hours of time that neither Krissi nor I can account for. One minute it was 8:20 at night, the next minute it was 6:30 in the morning."

"So how do you know you weren't dreaming?"

Philip tried to smile. "What I saw last night—the lights, the field, the burning trees—it was no dream."

Ryan frowned. "How can you be so sure?" He turned to Krissi. "And you don't remember any of it?"

"Not yet," Krissi said. "But I talked to the Ascension Lady, and she's going to hypnotize me and help me remember all the forgotten stuff."

Ryan and Becka exchanged uneasy glances. They remembered all too well what had happened when Becka had been hypnotized . . . and the way she'd almost been killed because of it.

Becka leaned forward. She had promised herself not to talk during the trip, and definitely not to preach, but this was important. "Krissi?"

The girl turned, giving her half an ear.

"Hypnotism is kind of tricky. Are you sure that's something you want to go through with?"

Krissi's expression hardened. "Please—"

But before she could continue, Philip hit the brakes and brought the Jeep to a sliding stop. "What in the world?"

"What's wrong?" Ryan asked.

"Up ahead . . . lying in the road."

Ryan and Becka craned their necks to see what looked like a cow.

"Is it dead?" Krissi asked.

"Looks like." Philip opened his door and stepped out.

Krissi followed. "See, I told you I saw a cow."

Ryan and Becka traded looks and climbed out after them.

"What's a cow doing all the way out here?" Ryan asked.

"That was my question," Philip said as he and Krissi continued in the lead. "In fact, that's exactly what I asked Krissi just before I saw the lights." They arrived at the cow and came to a stop. "Will you look at that." Ryan and Becka approached as Philip kneeled down to examine the carcass. "It's been gutted."

"What?" Ryan asked.

"See for yourself." Philip picked up a nearby stick and pushed a flap of skin aside. "All of its organs, they've been removed."

The four stared in silence.

"And look at those incisions," Ryan said,

kneeling down to join him. He motioned to the cut sections in the hide. "Look how clean they are."

Philip nodded. "They've been burned in, like with a laser or something."

Becka tried her best to stay calm, but once again she could feel an icy chill grip her shoulders. She looked up, searching the woods, peering down the road. Something was there. She knew it.

"You think someone, like, butchered it?" Krissi asked. "For the meat?"

"That's a possibility," Philip said.

Ryan shook his head. "I don't think so."

"Why not?"

"There's no blood. Do you see any blood around?"

The question brought Becka's attention back to the carcass. She searched the ground. Ryan was right. There wasn't a drop of blood to be found anywhere.

"Guys . . ." It was Krissi. Her voice sounded very thin, very frightened. Becka saw she was trembling and looking down the road. "I, uh, I don't . . . I don't think we should go any farther. I don't think we should go in there at all."

The other three looked at Krissi, exchanged glances, then followed her gaze down the road.

4

"*B*EAM ME UP, SCOTTY, BEAM ME UP! *SQUAWK.* BEAM ME UP!"

Scott reached over and stroked Cornelius with the eraser tip of his pencil. The parrot craned his neck this way and that, making sure Scott hit all the right spots.

Ah, ecstasy . . .

It was 5:30 P.M. Friday night. Scott didn't have to be at Hubert's for the next campaign of Crypts and Wizards until 7:00. On his desk was a tablet of carefully planned characteristics for the new and improved Ttocs. It had taken him most of the afternoon to create this new character, and for the most part he was happy.

For the most part.

Still . . . something was gnawing at him. He couldn't put his finger on it, but he was pretty sure it had something to do with the game. And with the way he had acted toward Bonnie Eagleman in geometry class.

He reached over to flip on the computer. A moment later he was in the chat room. He was hoping to connect with Z, the mysterious figure who had taken him and Becka under his wing. There seemed to be nothing Z didn't know—even in personal areas where he shouldn't know anything. That's what made him so interesting.

And, at times, so spooky.

Z didn't normally log on until 9:00 P.M., but from time to time he could be contacted earlier. Scott was hoping this would be one of those times. A moment later the screen came up, and he typed in his handle:

This is New Kid. Z, are you there?

He waited. Finally the words formed:

Hello, New Kid. Are you enjoying the game?

Scott sucked in his breath. No matter how many times Z pulled stunts like that, it still gave him the willies. He wanted to ask Z how he got his information, but he knew Z's response would be the same as always: silence.

Reluctantly, Scott plowed ahead with his next question:

What do you know about role-playing games?

The response came quickly:

I know there are several available and that they are quite engaging.

Scott nodded. Z had that right. He typed:

What about problems?
Have you ever heard of any?

There was a long pause. Scott typed:

Z, are you still there?

Finally a question appeared:

Do you find yourself relating too closely
with your created character?

Scott fought off another shiver and typed:

Maybe. How did you know?

It is quite common among fantasy role-playing
games. Psychologists have proven that extended
time of living in fantasy can make it difficult to
distinguish between fantasy and reality.

Scott felt himself growing defensive. He
typed:

That's only for children or the weak minded.

Perhaps, but Gary Gygax, the creator of one such
game, Dungeons & Dragons, is quoted as saying:
"You can get very emotionally involved. I've got
several characters I've nurtured through many
tension-filled, terror-fraught D&D games, and I'd
be really crushed if I lost one of them. They can
become very much a part of you."

Scott stared at the words, then typed:

But that doesn't make it unhealthy.

There was a pause. Finally:

50

Please stand by for data:

Scott knew Z was checking his resources. Sometimes this would take a few minutes, a day, or even a week. Not this time. This time the information appeared in just a few seconds:

The National Coalition on Television Violence has linked heavy involvement with the violence-oriented fantasy role-playing war games to over 90 deaths. These include 62 murders, 26 suicides, and 2 deaths of undetermined causes.

Scott studied the screen. More information appeared:

Psychiatrist Thomas E. Radecki states: "While perhaps a hundred young people have been led to murder and suicide, the evidence suggests that thousands have committed more minor anti-social behavior, and hundreds of thousands have become desensitized to violence."

Scott typed:

But I'm smarter than that. I'm not going to go out and kill somebody after playing Crypts and Wizards.

Probably not. However, if your created character
is involved in sex, violence, witchcraft, greed, or
any other type of immorality, a small part of you
actually participates with him in those acts.

Scott snorted.

It's just fantasy; it's just in my head.
I'm not really doing it.

What you frequently think, you start to become.

How can you say that?

It's a psychological fact. It's also in your Bible.

Where?

Christ states that if you hate someone,
it's as if you've committed murder. If you
lust after someone, it's as if you've
committed adultery.

Scott paused. It was true, that was basic
Sunday school info he'd heard all his life.
But still . . .

Z's final words appeared on the screen:

"For as [a man] thinks in his heart, so is HE"
(Proverbs 23:7). Good night, New Kid.

Scott stared at the verse, then glanced at his watch. 5:56. The game would start in an hour. He had to make a decision.

~~

Krissi continued gazing down the overgrown road. Becka could see she was trembling and moved to her side. "Are you all right? Krissi?"

She finally turned, but when her eyes met Becka's they had changed from wide-eyed fear to narrow, suspicious anger. "This is your doing, isn't it?"

Rebecca frowned. "What?"

"You're trying to frighten me. You're trying to stop me from making contact."

The others exchanged discreet glances. Philip cleared his throat and reached out to put his arm around her. "Krissi—"

She shrugged him off and continued glaring at Becka. "You know they're down that road, don't you? You know they're waiting for me, and you're trying to scare me off."

"Krissi," Philip repeated, "nobody's trying to do anything. If you don't want us to go any further, then we don't have t—"

She spun around to Philip, her eyes widening in surprise. "You're in on this, too?"

"What?"

She started backing away, looking first at

Philip, then Ryan, then Becka. "Why are you doing this? Why are you trying to stop me?"

Philip took a half step toward her. "Krissi, come on! Nobody's—"

"Liar!"

The accusation stopped him cold.

She looked over her shoulder, back down the road. From the look on her face, whatever was there both attracted and horrified her.

"Krissi . . ."

She took another step back. A look of determination filled her face.

Philip continued. "Krissi, please, you're acting really weird. You're scaring all of—"

Before he could finish she spun around and sprinted down the road.

"Krissi!" Philip was the first to start after her. "Come back!"

Ryan and Becka followed.

Krissi disappeared around the bend, but they knew she was still running. They could hear the brush rustling and twigs snapping.

"Krissi!" Philip's tone was both frantic and angry.

When they finally reached the bend and rounded it, they slowed to a stop. There, before them, was the field. The field Philip had described. But Krissi was nowhere in sight. Obviously she had left the road. But which direction had she taken?

"Krissi!" Philip shouted. "Krissi, answer me!"

There was no sound, only the group's heavy breathing. Becka reached out to touch Ryan's shoulder, directing his attention across the field, to the left side . . . to a stand of burned trees. The charred trunks looked like poles, the bare branches reached out like blackened skeleton arms.

"See?" Philip said, nodding. "It's exactly like I told you. No way was it a dream."

The three continued to stare until Becka motioned for them to be still. "Listen."

They did. There was a scratching, digging sound.

Philip shouted, "Krissi? Krissi, is that you?"

No answer. Only more digging.

Becka pointed. "It's coming from the trees."

They started through the tall grass toward the burned trees. Becka wasn't sure whether her heart was pounding from excitement or fear. She had no time to decide. Immediately they came upon a long strip of burned grass about five feet wide.

Philip slowed to a stop. They took his cue. "This is the path the beam of light cut. It started at those trees and ran all the way to my Jeep."

Ryan stooped to the ground. He picked up a piece of burnt wood and gave a sniff.

The digging sound resumed. It was louder

than before and mixed with another sound. Gasping grunts.

"Krissi!" Philip started up the charcoal path toward the trees. Ryan and Becka followed. A moment later they arrived under the trees and discovered Krissi. She was on her knees, holding a large stick, and digging and drawing in the blackened dirt. With each stroke of the stick she grunted and groaned.

"Krissi . . ." Philip dropped to her side, but she did not notice. She was in another world, too preoccupied to notice anyone or anything. Her clothes were covered in ash, her face smeared with charcoal.

"Krissi . . ." Philip grabbed hold of her shoulders. She continued drawing. He shook her. "Krissi!" Still no response. "Krissi, listen to me!" The shaking knocked the stick from her grasp, but she did not stop. She dropped onto her hands and began clawing the dirt with her fingers, grunting and groaning like an animal.

"Krissi!" He forced her to look at him. "Can you hear me? Can you hear me?!"

She blinked. Once, twice . . .

"Krissi!"

Recognition slowly filled her eyes. She looked at the others, her expression lost and confused.

"Are you all right?" Philip asked, his voice husky with concern and fear.

Suddenly, she threw her arms around him, clinging to him for all she was worth. "Help me," she gasped. "Don't let me go again! Don't let me go!"

"It's OK," he comforted. "We're here. We're here."

She began sobbing. "Don't let me go. . . . Don't let me go. . . ."

"Shh, it's OK. You're not going anywhere. Shh . . ."

Rebecca looked on. She wanted desperately to help but knew there was nothing she could do. It wasn't until Ryan touched her arm and pointed toward the drawing in the dirt and ash that her concern gave way to another emotion. The markings were several inches deep. Only now it was clear they were not drawings. They were words.

WE AWAIT AT CABIN.

Over at Hubert's, Scott stared at the screen as the Crypt Master took roll, typing each of the players' names.

Arzule?

57

Present.

Wraith?

Here.

The game was about to begin. Scott was more than a little uneasy about being there, especially after talking with Z. But he'd gone to so much work preparing and perfecting his character, he couldn't just quit now. Not until he saw how well the new and improved Ttocs performed.

The roll call continued.

Ashram?

Here.

Scott had decided he would play one more game, that was all. Just one more. Only this one he'd play as Darryl had suggested: with everything he had, with his heart, his mind, and his soul. If he lost, fine. He'd walk away knowing he'd given it his best shot.

Quantoz?

Yo.

Drucid?

Here.

If he won, so much the better. He could walk away knowing he had beaten the Master. But to stop after his first defeat . . . well, let's face it, that just wasn't Scott Williams's style.

Phantasm?

Here.

He trusted Z, of course, but what Z had written was still one man's opinion. And it wasn't like there was some specific verse in the Bible that said, "Thou shall not play Crypts and Wizards."

Shredder?

I'm here.

Ttocs?

Scott stared at the screen. His name appeared again.

Ttocs?

Scott continued to hesitate. If he was going to play this thing, he was going to play all out. He heard a loud sniff to his right and Darryl's squeaky voice.

"Scott, you're up."

He nodded.

Ttocs?

He reached for the keyboard and slowly typed:

Present.

There. It was done. One more time. And this time he was going to play for all he was worth.

5

"There he is."

Becka turned to see Philip exiting Krissi's house. He spotted their car and headed down the walk to join them. Rebecca rolled down her window. The night air was chilly but not cold. It looked like rain. Of course. It always rained on weekends.

"Is she OK?" Becka asked.

Philip ducked his head through the window and rested his arms on the door. "Yeah, she'll be OK. Pretty tired though." He glanced away, trying to sound casual. "'Course she wants to see the Ascension Lady tomorrow. You know, get hypnotized, find out what really happened and everything . . ."

Becka nodded. She wanted to say something, but her last comment on hypnotism had nearly caused a fight.

"When she wrote *cabin,*" Ryan asked, "any idea what she meant?"

Philip shrugged. "Maybe her folks' cabin."

"At Cougar Creek?"

"Maybe." Silence stole over the conversation.

"You going to be all right?" Becka asked.

Philip forced a smile, but there was no missing his concern. It was obvious he really loved the girl. "Sure."

More silence.

"Listen, uh—" he cleared his throat—"I really appreciate you guys being there for her tonight. I know she hasn't been the nicest person to be around, especially to you two."

Ryan shrugged. "No prob."

Philip continued, "I haven't said much . . . but, well, you need to know that I really respect your guys' faith and stuff."

Becka watched him struggle to put his feelings into words.

"I mean, what you've got—your belief in God and all that, it's pretty cool . . . and sometimes, I, uh, well, I envy you."

Before she could catch herself, Becka quietly laid her hand on his arm. It was a small gesture, but she saw it was one he appreciated.

"Anyway, maybe, when you pray and stuff, maybe you could say a little prayer for her, too."

Becka nodded.

"Philip?" Ryan asked.

He looked over to him.

"You could join us if you wanted. In praying, I mean."

There was that smile again. Sad. Tired. "Thanks," he said, "but I was there once . . . remember?"

Ryan looked at him and nodded.

Another moment of silence.

"Well," Philip finally pulled from the window, forcing another grin and trying to bring the conversation to a happy ending. "You guys take care, and we'll let you know what happens tomorrow."

But Ryan wouldn't let go that easily. Philip had just shared his heart with them, and he wasn't going to slip away that easily. "Philip?"

He stooped back down. Ryan's voice was

gentle and quiet. "He's still there for you, man. All you have to do is reach out. He's still there."

Philip's grin faded as he searched Ryan's eyes. His friend was speaking straight from the heart, and he knew it. Finally he nodded. "I know. . . ."

With that he rose from the window and started toward the Jeep.

Becka watched him cross to the driver's side and open the door. "What did he mean, he'd been there?" she asked. "Been where?"

"Philip used to believe in God . . . a long time ago. His whole family."

She turned to Ryan. "Philip?"

Ryan nodded, watching as Philip climbed into the Jeep and started up the engine.

"What happened?"

"His folks divorced. He stopped believing in God." He shrugged. "He stopped believing in anything."

Becka felt like she'd been hit in the stomach. Her heart leaped out to the boy as she turned and watched his Jeep pull into the street, then head down the road. "That's terrible."

Ryan nodded.

They watched the taillights disappear into the night as rain started splattering on their windshield.

Scott stared at the screen.

The dice had been good to him. Very good. He'd scored enough points to purchase plenty of weapons, spells, armor, poisons, and hexes at the Wizard's Shoppe. Not only had Ttocs become one of the biggest and most powerful players, but thanks to Scott's careful planning, he was also one of the most ruthless. Already he had severely crippled one player and completely disemboweled a mischievous warlock. But that was only the beginning.

It was his turn, and once again he chose "Combat." This time against Darryl's character, Drucid.

"Oh, man!" Darryl gave a loud sniff from beside him. "Why pick on me? Look how weak I am. I'm no threat."

That didn't matter to the bloodthirsty Ttocs.

They rolled, and Ttocs began the attack.

First he hit Drucid with a mace, a spiked metal ball on a chain. Drucid was able to hold off the first couple of blows, but his armor was like paper when pitted against the mighty Ttocs. He soon began to crumple.

"Give me a break," Darryl moaned.

Scott barely heard. He wanted to save his armor points for another encounter, so he released his pet vampire, Rabid, to continue the assault.

Drucid tried to run for cover, but the dice worked against him. He'd barely turned before Rabid swooped down out of the sky, slashed into his neck, and began gulping Drucid's steamy black blood.

Scott could see Darryl fidgeting beside him. It was obvious Drucid's life would be over before it had a chance to begin. "Come on!" Darryl whispered. "You gotta let me play a little longer."

Scott glanced at him with a sly grin. No way did he intend to let up. He rolled for another attack. Once again he won. Now Ttocs began a brutal karate assault on Drucid. The creature was able to deflect the kicks and punches, but he didn't see the dagger Ttocs had hidden in his belt . . . until he felt its icy blade slip between his ribs. Drucid staggered. Ttocs threw him into a headlock. And there, with his bare hands, Ttocs crushed Drucid's skull like an egg.

Darryl groaned and stared at his laptop. It was over. Just like that. His character was dead.

Darryl was definitely not happy.

Scott, on the other hand, was ecstatic. The rush of excitement was so great that his fingers were actually trembling. What a game!

Ttocs had just annihilated another victim. Gloriously. Ruthlessly. But there were plenty more. Scott grinned with glee.

Ttocs was unstoppable. He would not be held back.

~

It was Rebecca and Ryan's turn with Z. Since it was Friday, Mom had no problem with Becka having late-night company, just as long as the door stayed open and they said good-bye by midnight. Becka had already logged on to the computer, connected with Z, and started asking questions about Krissi and UFOs.

But are they real? UFOs, I mean?

Evidence indicates that all but 5% of reported sightings have a normal, logical explanation.

And the other 5%? Are they really spaceships from outer space?

Yes and no.

Please explain.

Most reputable researchers believe the appearances are real, but not physical.

I don't understand.

If they are physical, they would have
to follow physical laws.

Such as?

1. Most sightings have been reported to travel
between 1,000 and 18,000 miles an hour. Yet
no person has ever reported hearing a loud boom.

Ryan nodded. "He's right. The speed of
sound is around seven hundred miles an
hour. Anything traveling faster than that
would create a sonic boom."
Z continued:

2. The objects are often seen coming
to instant stops.

Why is that a problem?

What happens when you are inside a car traveling
at 20 or 30 miles an hour and it suddenly stops?

You get thrown forward.

Imagine that same effect if you were traveling
several thousand times faster.

Your body would be trashed?

"Hamburger city," Ryan chuckled.
Z wasn't finished.

3. Many UFOs are seen streaking across the sky,
then making abrupt right-angle turns.

Becka typed:

*Wouldn't the same thing happen? Whoever was
inside would be destroyed.*

Correct. The force of making a right-angle turn
while traveling at only 5,000 miles an hour is
strong enough to shear in half a solid steel ball, let
alone destroy any living creature inside.

So what are they really?

Most researchers believe UFOs are not
extraterrestrial but inner-dimensional.

Meaning?

They don't come from other worlds; they come
from other dimensions.

Becka swallowed hard. She didn't like the
sound of that. Slowly she typed:

The only other dimension we know is the spiritual world. Are you saying these things are spiritual?

UFO author Michael Lindemann is quoted as saying that Dr. Jacques Valle, the leading UFO researcher in the world, believes that "so-called aliens don't fit any logical pattern of extra-terrestrial visitors." Tracing back through the long history of reported humanoid superbeings in religious and folkloric literature, he suggests that today's aliens might be a modern analogy to ancient gods, demons, and fairies.

Becka tried to swallow again, but this time there was nothing left to swallow. The word *demon* stuck out like a flashing road sign. She typed:

Those are just opinions, right?

Expert opinions. Consider the following points: 1. Most "alien" messages are autowritten or spoken through humans in exactly the same method that occultists use to channel demons. 2. Their messages frequently emphasize the nondeity of Jesus Christ. 3. They generally insist man will never be judged by God. 4. Many of these channelers experience the exact physical and mental symptoms of people who are possessed by demons: nausea, hallucination, antisocial behavior, and hearing voices.

Ryan leaned back in his chair. "He's describing Krissi to a T."

Becka nodded and was already typing:

What about people who claim they've been taken by aliens?

Reports of so-called alien abductions are increasing. However, it is interesting that every abducted person I've studied has had previous involvement with the occult.

Ryan moaned, "Krissi again."

Becka nodded and continued typing:

Every one has dabbled in the occult?

Without exception.

Becka was almost finished, but she had one last question:

What sort of things happen in an abduction?

Sometimes the person is returned physically injured. Sometimes not. But there are always psychological scars. Worst of all, once an abduction happens, the victims frequently find themselves being taken over and over again.

Becka and Ryan stared at one another. Each knew what the other was thinking. If it had happened to Krissi once, it would probably happen again.

6

*P*hilip sat, nervous and edgy, in the back room of the Ascension Bookshop. The room was full of shadows. A couple of worn sofas were shoved against the maroon walls, which were decorated with astrological signs. This was the meeting room of the Society, a group of kids who dabbled in the occult. Philip had heard about them, but he'd never taken them seriously. Come to think of it, he had never taken the Ascension Lady or this bookshop too seriously, either.

Until now.

Now the woman had Krissi sitting in a chair and in some sort of trance.

Philip didn't like that. Not that he was a control freak—Krissi was free to do whatever she wanted—but he had always been there to protect and defend her. Not this time. This time there was nothing he could do except sit and listen as she recalled the logging road, the cow, the lights, the fire, and stepping out of the Jeep.

Beads of perspiration covered her face as she gasped for breath. "I'm hanging on to the mirror. I'm screaming to Philip, 'Don't let go; don't let me go, please don't let me go!'"

The room seemed to be charged with electricity, but the Ascension Lady kept her voice even and calm. "And then what happened?"

Suddenly Krissi burst into tears.

Philip rose to his feet, but the Ascension Lady motioned for him to stay back. "It's OK," she reassured him in a whisper. "This is what she has been repressing; this is what her subconscious needs to uncover."

"Philip . . ." Krissi's voice sounded very far away, like a lost little girl.

"What happened?" the Ascension Lady asked. "Where's Philip?"

Tears streamed down Krissi's cheeks. "He let go. He let go of me. . . ."

The accusation—the idea she would think he let go on purpose—cut deep into Philip's heart. He wanted to set the record straight, to tell her he'd hung on as long as he could, but the Ascension Lady's look told him to remain quiet.

Suddenly Krissi's face filled with horror. "No! Stay away, stay away from me!"

"Where are you?" the Ascension Lady asked. "Where are you now?"

"I'm inside. The light, it pulled me inside. They're all around me."

"Who is? Who is all around?"

"Stay back!"

"Who are they, Krissi? What do they look like?"

"Their eyes! They're so big . . . like insects. Black. Shiny. Stay away!"

Philip started to stand again, but the Ascension Lady threw him another quelling look. "What else?" she continued. "What else can you tell us about them?"

"No hair. Big heads, like upside-down tear-drops. Two little holes for a nose. And their mouths, they don't have any lips, just a thin line."

"How many of them do you see?"

"Six . . . no, eight. They're short. Four feet.

And they're so skinny, just skin stretched over bone. Gray skin and bones."

"Gray? You said gray?"

"Yes."

"Are you certain they are gray?"

"Is that common?" Philip whispered.

The Ascension Lady nodded.

"Yes," Krissi said. "Smooth, powdery gray. Like they've never even seen the sun." Suddenly she cocked her head as if listening. "What? What do you mean?"

"What's happening now?"

"One of them is talking. He's telling me not to worry. They've come to help us, to help me." Again her expression changed. "No . . . no! Stay away. No, please."

"Krissi, what's happening?"

"They're touching me. Their fingers are long and skinny. They only have three on each hand. No, please . . . I'm not ready for this. Please, you're scaring me."

"Krissi?"

"No!" Krissi tossed her head first one way, then the other. "No, please . . ." She gulped in air as if she were fighting.

"Krissi, what's going on?"

No answer.

"Krissi, talk to me."

Her thrashing increased. Back and forth. Sweat streamed down her face.

"Krissi, what—?"

"They're taking off my vest. No! I try to fight, but my arms, they've done something to my arms! I can't move my arms! No! *NO!*" Her whole body writhed and convulsed, but her arms stayed perfectly limp at her side. "No . . . no!"

That was it. Philip had to do something. He lunged from his seat and rushed to her side.

"Krissi!"

The Ascension Lady reached out to grasp his arm, shaking her head fiercely. "You'll only make it worse!" she hissed. She turned back to Krissi, fighting to keep her voice calm. "Krissi, can you hear me?"

"Machines . . . they've got machines. They're all over me. The machines are touching me everywhere. No. No! Make them stop. Please make them stop!" She shuddered, her face contorting in pain. "Nooo . . ."

"That's enough!" Philip shouted.

The Ascension Lady shook her head without looking at him. "No, it's important she—"

"I said that's *enough!*"

"She's there," the woman argued. "This is what happened. You can't just—"

"Augh!"

They spun to see Krissi shrieking at the top of her lungs. *"AUGHHHHH!"*

Philip knelt beside her. The Ascension

Lady tried to block him, but he pushed her aside. He grasped Krissi's arms and shook her. "Krissi! Krissi, wake up!"

She continued to fight and struggle and cry.

"Krissi, it's Philip." He shook her again, harder. "It's me! Krissi, wake up."

"No . . . no . . . please . . ."

"Krissi—"

Suddenly her body went limp. She was still gasping for breath, but apparently whatever she had seen was gone.

Philip touched her face gently, not even noticing the way his hand trembled. "Krissi . . . can you hear me? Krissi?"

Her eyes fluttered, then opened. They darted back and forth as she tried to get her bearings. Once she realized where she was, her face scrunched into a frown. "Why did you stop me?" Her voice was hoarse from the screaming.

"What?"

"You stopped me. Why did you stop me? They were giving me instructions. They were telling me—" She stopped, noticing the Ascension Lady behind him. "Why did you let him stop me?"

The woman only shook her head.

Krissi's eyes shifted back to Philip. "We've got to go."

"What? Where?"

"My folks' cabin. Cougar Creek."

Philip scowled.

"It's too crowded here. Too many interferences. They want me to meet them at Cougar Creek, where it's isolated, where we can be alone."

"Krissi, that's a two-hour drive into the mountains. We can't—"

"They want to give me more information. They said I need further instruct—"

"After all you've been through?" Philip exploded. He'd had enough. "No way. It's over."

She met his eyes. He felt a chill at the icy glare. There was a determination in her eyes that he'd never seen before.

"If you won't go with me," she said, "I'll go by myself." She started to rise from her seat, but she was a little shaky.

"Whoa." the Ascension Lady moved in to steady her.

"I'm fine," Krissi said, pushing her aside. "I'm fine." Then turning to look at Philip squarely, she asked, "So are you coming, or am I going alone?"

Twenty minutes later Becka hung up the phone. She'd just talked to a very nervous and very worried Philip.

"I don't know what's going on," he'd said.

"But . . . we can't face this thing on our own. We need your help. Can you and Ryan come to Cougar Creek? Can you meet us there? We really need you guys."

Rebecca's first instinct was to say no. The last thing in the world she wanted was to face more spiritual warfare. It had only been a week or so since her last encounter. An encounter that had left Julie, her best friend, still in bed, recovering.

And if that cow, the burned grass in the field, and the destroyed trees were any indication of the power she would have to face . . . well, who could blame Becka for thinking overtime to find an excuse not to go.

If only Philip hadn't sounded so . . . frightened.

She finally managed to hang up, but not before promising that she'd run it past her mother. With any luck Mom would freak at the idea of her and Ryan taking a two-hour drive into the mountains, and that would be that. With any luck Mom would encourage her to avoid any more spiritual encounters.

Then again, Mom was always full of surprises.

"I think you should go, Beck."

"What?"

"I think you and Ryan and Scotty need to go up there and help."

Becka followed her into the kitchen. "But, Mom . . ."

"I don't like the idea any better than you, but you said it yourself. They need you."

"But why . . ." She struggled for the words. "Why you?"

Becka nodded.

Mom turned to her. They'd had this conversation more than once. Her answer was gentle but firm. "I think you know the answer."

Becka looked down.

"You've known it for months. Even when Dad was alive, when we used to pray over you—even then we knew you would be called to something like this."

"But . . ." Becka could feel her throat tighten. She looked up at her mother. "I'm really scared."

Mom paused, then nodded. "Me too, sweetheart . . . me too. Every time you get involved in something like this, it makes me go cold inside." She turned as though she was looking out the kitchen window—but Becka knew she was trying to control her emotions. After a minute, Mom went on. "Believe me, if I had my way I'd say no. But . . . part of loving is letting go." Finally she turned to face Becka. "And part of trusting the Lord is letting go, too."

Becka looked into her mother's eyes.

Mom reached over and brushed her hair behind her ears. "He hasn't failed us yet, sweetheart. He won't fail you now."

Before she knew it, Becka had wrapped her arms around her mother. She loved this woman with all of her heart. She knew this was as hard on Mom as it was on her. She also knew she had a lot to learn from the woman—especially when it came to loving and trusting God.

Now she needed to talk to Scott.

"No way."

"Scotty, they need us."

"I'm busy."

Becka stayed on his heels all the way up the stairs and down the hall into his room. "Listen, what's going on at that cabin is a lot more important than some stupid game."

He snorted. "A lot you know."

Her voice raised a notch. "I know you've been like the invisible man ever since you started playing it."

He turned on her. "Is that some sort of crime?"

"It's a crime when there are people who need help and you'd rather sit around and play some stupid game."

"Stop calling it that!" The resentful outburst surprised them both. Scott continued, obviously forcing himself to calm down. "Listen, this is more than just a game, all right?"

Rebecca simply looked at him.

"It's . . . Beck, there's nothing like it. When I play, it's like . . . I don't know, it's like I've got this power, like I can do all these incredible things I could never do in real life."

"It's just a game, Scotty. Make-believe."

"I know, but sometimes . . . sometimes it seems so real. More than real. Like I'm really there. Like I'm really this guy with all this power." He shrugged and turned to stroke the sleeping Cornelius. "I just don't feel like giving it up. Especially for some wild-goose chase up in the mountains."

Becka continued to stare. This was not like her brother. Not at all. He was always the first to jump in and help people. "Scotty, we're talking about real people here. Real flesh-and-blood people who need our help. Mine. *And* yours."

He fidgeted. "You don't need me. You've done it before without me."

She shook her head slowly, her expression thoughtful, almost apprehensive. "This is different. This one is really different." She looked at him. "We need you there."

He glanced up at her. She held his gaze.

He looked over to the computer, and Becka could see wheels starting to turn.

"Hold on," he said. "Wait a minute. . . . Who says I can't do both?"

"What?"

"Sure. Darryl's got his laptop and he's out of the game."

"What's that got to—"

"There's a telephone up there, right?"

"Yeah, I suppose."

"I bet I could call in and hook up with the modem. Then I can play from wherever we're at."

"Scotty, I don't think that's exactly what—" She broke off. Scott wasn't listening. He was picking up the phone and dialing Darryl's number. Becka stood, watching. She wasn't too sure this was a good idea.

Still, having part of Scott there was better than having none of him. . . .

She watched the excitement on his face as Darryl agreed to loan him the laptop, and a chill of doubt ran through her.

. . . or was it?

Shaking off her concern, she looked at her watch. It was 3:05. As soon as Scott was off the phone she'd call Ryan. They could be on the road within an hour.

7

*S*cott knew something was wrong. Here he was, riding in the backseat of Ryan's Mustang, going up into the mountains for some sort of major showdown with some sort of major evil, and all he could think about was what Ttocs's next move would be in the game. Amazing. Part of him knew Becka was right when she said it was just a game. But part of him knew it went much deeper than that. Much, much deeper . . .

For the hundredth time he shuffled through Darryl's laptop computer case to make sure he had everything necessary to call up on the modem. And for the hundredth time he asked Ryan about the phone situation. "You're absolutely sure Krissi's folks don't have a telephone?"

"Will you relax," Ryan chuckled. "The General Store is just ahead. I guarantee you, the owner will let you call from there."

"It can't be a pay phone. It's got to be a line I can plug in to the computer."

"He's cool. I'm sure he'll let you use the store phone just as long as you pay for it and don't take too long."

"It won't be long. Just a few minutes every half hour or so."

"Every half hour?" Becka turned to Scott from the front. "How long do you plan to spend there?"

That was the question Scott had been dreading. Fortunately, Ryan slowed the car and was turning into the General Store's parking lot. A perfect time to change the subject. "Are we here?" he asked.

"This is the place."

It was an old-fashioned store with rough

wood planking and a long front porch. The
sun was just thinking about setting, and the
warm glow of the lights inside looked invit-
ing. Even more so when they stepped out
into the cold.

"It's freezing!" Becka shivered as she fumbled with the buttons on her coat.

Ryan grinned. White plumes of smoke
escaped from his mouth as he spoke to Scott.
"The cabin is just a mile or so up the road.
There's this big orange trout for a mailbox,
and the driveway winds up a little hill. You
can't miss it."

Scott nodded.

"Well, let's get you settled," Ryan said
as he started up the store's steps. "How long
did you say? A few minutes every half
hour?"

Scott nodded, doing his best to avoid
Becka's glare. He knew he was cheating. He
knew by agreeing to come he'd led her to
believe he'd help. Well, he would. Sort of.
He hoped. He readjusted the computer strap
on his shoulder and headed up the stairs
after them.

~

"What a jerk," Becka said as they pulled out
of the store's parking lot and onto the road.
"He won't even stop long enough to help.

It's like that stupid game's got a hold on him."

Ryan nodded. "I had a friend that really got caught up into that stuff, too."

"What happened?"

"He just sort of dropped out."

"Dropped out?"

"I still see him around school and stuff, but it's like he's not really there. Like, he's in a different world."

Becka turned to look back at the store as it disappeared around the bend. Her anger and frustration had already turned to concern.

~

Becka and Ryan had barely left the store before Scott had situated himself in the back office and connected with Hubert's computer. The other players in the group had agreed to let him accumulate turns while he traveled, so when he finally got on-line, Scott was ready to give it everything he had. Unfortunately, the dice had other ideas.

On his first move Ttocs was attacked by a living corpse. The hideous creature began shredding his flesh and devouring it. Each time Scott rolled the dice for a counterattack, he lost. Each time he tried to defend himself, he gave up more and more of his power.

Things were not going well. Not well at all.

Finally, through a complicated incantation, Ttocs was able to conjure up a fireball. The light exploded in all directions, raining flames down upon the undead monster and sending it scurrying for cover. But the damage was already done. Ttocs was far weaker than when he'd started.

And still they came at him. This time it was one of the players. Ttocs had barely taken a step before the infamous Quantoz, an offspring of Satan himself, went in for the kill. It was unbelievable the way the dice kept rolling against Scott. Each time Ttocs tried to defend himself, he lost. And each time he lost, Scott grew more and more depressed.

Finally Quantoz's turn was over. Nearly half of Ttocs's armor had been depleted and almost all of his magic had been neutralized. It had been a bloody series of attacks, but at least for now it was over.

Scott leaned back in the office chair and rubbed his neck. His face was wet with perspiration, and he was breathing hard. "Just a game," Becka had said. Hardly. Not when he was fighting for his life. And it was his life. Ttocs was his creation. Ttocs was a part of him . . . Ttocs *was* him.

But that was OK. His turn wouldn't be for several more minutes. He would have time to rest, to get his bearings and, now that he was so much weaker, find a way to stay in the game without being destroyed.

Suddenly his thoughts were interrupted by another player signaling to attack him. It was obvious the player thought he might be able to finish Ttocs off. Maybe he could.

Scott took a deep breath and sat up at the keyboard preparing for another assault. . . .

"Here we go." Ryan turned left onto a dirt road and started winding up the steep, tree-lined driveway. The sun had just set and the temperature was dropping quickly.

"How do you know about this place?" Becka asked.

"Krissi's folks used to invite us up every summer. Me, Julie, Krissi, and Philip."

Becka nodded, once again remembering how she was the new kid. Once again feeling like the outsider, the one who had come in and ruined everything. As if reading her thoughts, Ryan reached out and took her hand. She gratefully accepted it. It was warm, strong, and reassuring.

At last the cabin came into view. It was one story, not too big, and covered with worn brown shingles. Philip's Jeep sat in front.

"That's weird," Ryan said.

"What?"

"The chimney, there's no smoke coming from it. In this weather you'd think they would have started a fire. It's the only way to heat the cabin."

"And check out the Jeep," Becka said, pointing toward it. Both doors were wide open. Ryan pulled up alongside it, turned off the ignition, and climbed out. "Philip? Krissi?"

Becka followed, feet crunching on frozen gravel, clouds of breath hovering above her head. They looked inside the Jeep, but it held no clues. Just the usual guy clutter and—

"Ryan—" she motioned to the passenger seat—"it's Krissi's bag."

Ryan nodded, barely listening.

"You don't understand. Krissi would never go anywhere without her bag. It's got her makeup, her brush, all the bare essentials for her life."

Ryan stared down at it a moment. Then they both turned to the cabin. It looked completely deserted. No lights. No sign of activity. Once again Ryan reached out to take her hand—and once again Becka was grateful for its warmth and strength.

They started forward. This time it was Becka's turn to call out. "Krissi? Philip?"

No answer.

They arrived at the porch steps. The railing was covered with a thin layer of frost.

"Krissi!"

The air was dead still. No sound, no movement. Just the shuffling of their feet and the creaking wood as they started up the stairs.

"Philip!"

They reached the door. Ryan looked at Becka, took a deep breath, and reached for the handle. Becka wasn't sure if the shiver that raced across her shoulders was from the cold or from what awaited them inside.

She would soon find out.

8

A wave of relief washed over Philip as he heard Ryan and Becka calling his name outside the cabin. He wanted to shout an answer, but he was afraid to send Krissi into another fit. The last one had wiped her out. They had barely arrived when she had suddenly jumped out of the Jeep, run into the cabin, and thrown herself down on the floor, screaming. It was like an epileptic seizure, only worse.

It had taken all of Philip's strength just to stop her from crashing into the furniture and walls and hurting herself. When she had finally reached exhaustion, he did his best to quiet her. Soon her screams had turned to soft, helpless whimpering.

"Philip," she'd moaned, "I need a pencil—they need to write something. Please, get me a pencil."

But he had no pen or pencil on him, and he wasn't about to leave her to find one.

"Please, they want to communicate. We've got to let them communicate."

"Shh," was all he could say as he sat with her on the floor. Holding her. Rocking her. "Shh, it's going to be OK." He fought back the tears. It had been a long, long time since he had cried. But he was scared. More scared than he could remember—not of UFOs or aliens or whatever, but of losing Krissi. He'd lost his mother and sisters. That had nearly destroyed him. He wasn't about to lose the only other thing he cherished.

They stayed that way, huddled together on the floor, for he didn't know how long. It was freezing, but he didn't dare let go of her to start a fire. At least not yet. Maybe after she fell asleep. She was so exhausted she was nearly there.

Then he heard Ryan and Becka calling.

The cabin door creaked open and there they stood.

"Over here," he called softly. "We're over here."

Ryan was the first to step inside. "Are you guys OK?" He fumbled for the switch on the wall and snapped it on. Welcome light flooded the room. Becka entered behind him, but as soon as her foot touched the floor, Philip felt Krissi's body grow rigid.

"Who-who's there?" she asked, squinting from the light.

"It's us, Krissi," Ryan answered. "Me and Beck."

She looked up to Philip accusingly. "You told them where we were? You invited them?"

It was time to face the music. "Krissi, I don't think what's happening . . . I'm not convinced it's good."

"They'll scare him off!" She struggled to sit up. "You read what Xandrak wrote. He won't be able to help us if their beliefs hold us back."

"Maybe holding us back . . ." Philip searched for the words. "Maybe that's not such a bad idea."

"What?"

"After all that's happened to us, maybe there's something about their beliefs we need."

"How can you *say* that?" Her voice rang with hurt and betrayal. "They're going to ruin everything. Don't you see?"

"Krissi," Ryan said, "we're not here to ruin—"

But he was interrupted by his car horn honking in short bursts, over and over again. Everyone turned toward the open door. Outside, bright lights flashed on the trees, off and on, off and on.

"What's that?" Krissi demanded.

"I think it's my car alarm." Ryan stepped outside for a better look. "That's weird."

"Something bump into it?" Becka asked, joining him.

Ryan shook his head. "I never armed it. How could the thing go off if I never set it?" He shrugged, stuffed his hands into his pockets, and headed down the steps to investigate. Becka followed.

Philip wanted to call out, to beg them to stay. But he knew how weak and stupid that would sound, so he remained quiet.

He wished he hadn't.

As soon as Ryan and Becka were out of sight, Krissi rose unsteadily to her feet.

"Where are you going?"

"He's here," she whispered.

Immediately Philip was beside her. "Who is? Who's here?"

"Xandrak."

He fought off a shiver and looked around the room. "I don't see any—"

Suddenly the table radio blasted on at full volume. Philip spun toward it, but no one was there. He looked back at Krissi. She was staring off into space again, her eyes starting to glaze over. He gave her a little shake. "Krissi? Oh, not again! What's going on?"

She didn't respond.

The TV on the bookshelf suddenly came on and began to blare. There was no picture, just lots of snow. And static. Very loud static.

"Krissi?" He shouted over the noise. He gave her a harder shake. "Krissi!"

But Krissi didn't even seem to hear him. She slowly turned toward the door.

"Krissi! Answer me!"

No response.

"Ryan!" he shouted, more alarmed than ever. "Becka!"

Instantly the radio and TV shut off. Along with the light in the room. Once again they were immersed in darkness. And silence. Even Ryan's car alarm had stopped.

"Krissi?" Philip whispered.

Still no answer, but he could feel her body start to tremble.

"Krissi?"

Then, ever so slowly, she raised her hand

until it was pointing directly at the door. Philip's eyes followed her gesture; then he sucked in his breath. Someone was there. Standing in the open doorway. It was impossible to make out much detail, but there was a silhouette of a short creature, maybe four feet tall. He was grotesquely skinny with long arms and a strange, triangle-shaped head.

"Xandrak?" Krissi's voice was barely a whisper.

The creature said nothing but raised his arm. At the end of it were three long, wiry fingers.

Krissi started to move. Philip's grip on her shoulder tightened.

"Philip . . ."

He held her firmly.

"Philip, let me go. He wants to talk to me."

But he held tight. Nothing would make him let go. Not this time.

Without warning, there was an explosion of light. It blasted through the doorway and windows. Blinding. Overpowering. Exactly the same light that had assaulted them in the Jeep. The energy was so strong it knocked Philip to the ground. He barely hit the floor before he was scrambling to his knees, fighting to get back to his feet and grab Krissi. But by the time he stood, she was gone. He spun to the door. So was the creature.

"Krissi!" he screamed.

The light vanished.

"No!" He bolted toward the door and out onto the porch just in time to crash into Ryan.

"What was *that?*" Ryan exclaimed. "It was like lightning!"

"They've got Krissi!"

"Who? What?"

Then Philip spotted it. For a split second a ball of silvery light hovered over the ridge of the driveway—and then it was gone. There was no time to explain. He raced for his car.

Ryan grabbed him. "Philip, wait!"

"They have Krissi. Don't you understand?"

"Yes, but—"

"Let me go."

"You can't fight this stuff on your own."

He tried to pull away, but Ryan held him tight. "You don't understand!" Philip shouted. "I let her down once. I can't do it again!"

"You've got to let us help you!" Ryan shouted back. "You can't fight it on your own." Again Philip tried to break free, but Ryan held on. "You said it yourself. You need our help. You need our faith."

"I tried it."

"This is different."

They continued to struggle. "Let go!"

"Philip, you've got to trust—"

"Let go!"

"Phil—"

Philip clenched his fist, drew his arm back, and hit Ryan with everything he had. Becka screamed as Ryan flew across the porch, hitting the window with the back of his head. The glass shattered, and he slowly slid to the floor.

Philip did not stop to watch.

~

Ttocs's new attacker, Wraith, was a ghoul, fifteenth class. Normally he wouldn't waste time on someone as weak and defenseless as Ttocs had become, but Scott had been pretty ruthless in the beginning, and what goes around comes around. It was payback time.

The dice fell worse than before. Wraith relentlessly stripped Ttocs of his armor and weapon points, smashing, parrying, and dissolving them with deadly acid from his fangs.

Scott hunched over the keyboard in the back room of the store, typing for all he was worth. Sweat dripped from his face, but he didn't notice. His heart pounded furiously, but he didn't care. It was no longer his sweat or his heart. It was Ttocs's. And he was no longer in the General Store; he was somewhere in the crypt, fighting for his very life.

He rolled the dice to retreat, but Wraith was far too clever. He cast a spell on Ttocs, paralyzing him. Then, assisted by the powers of hell, he levitated Ttocs and turned him around, forcing him to face a giant sword made of dragon teeth. Teeth that would embed themselves into an opponent's throat and eat his flesh.

The sword flew swiftly toward his neck. Ttocs tried to move, to duck, but the spell was too powerful. The sword hit its mark. Scott cried out in pain, grabbing at his own throat. Now the teeth began their deadly job, gnawing and tearing. Ttocs gasped for breath, but it did no good. He staggered and clutched at his neck, coughing and wheezing. Everything around him started to spin, the light grew dim, color faded.

He fell. Hard. Try as he might, Scott could not get him to move. His unbeatable creation lay motionless.

It was over. Ttocs was dead.

Scott stared at the screen, his heart thundering in his head, his breath coming in short gasps. It couldn't be! Ttocs was too great. Scott had spent too much time making him powerful, unstoppable, undefeatable. But there on the screen lay the character, his eyes frozen in what had been a brutal, agonizing death.

Scott closed his own eyes. How could this

be? How could Ttocs be gone? He lowered his head into his hands as a lump of emotion rose into his throat. His friend was dead. His creation. His self . . .

Scott sat there silently a long, long time. And then he began to weep.

Philip bounced out of the driveway and slid onto the main road. He tromped on the gas and the Jeep fishtailed. He fought the wheel and managed to bring it back under control. A hundred yards ahead, the silvery ball of light hovered ten, maybe fifteen, feet above the road. It seemed to be waiting for him to catch up. Philip was happy to oblige.

He pushed harder on the accelerator. But as he picked up speed, so did the light. It was the same cat-and-mouse game they'd played before. The faster he went, the faster it went. Philip barely saw the road. He kept his eyes fixed on the object. It was hard to make out its exact size and shape. Sometimes it seemed as round as a ball, maybe seven feet across. Other times it looked like a flattened saucer, twenty feet in diameter.

But none of that mattered. All Philip knew was that somehow, some way, Krissi was a part of that light—and somehow, some way, he had to help her.

They hit the bend in the road. It curved to the right. He straightened it by cutting into the other lane. The General Store lay ahead. He screamed past it, doing between sixty and seventy miles an hour.

Suddenly, just past the store, the light took a hard left and disappeared into a newly cut driveway that wound deep into the woods.

Philip hit the brakes. Immediately he knew he'd made a mistake. The damp fog had frozen, leaving a thin, icy glaze on the road.

The Jeep started to slide.

Everything turned to slow motion. He could feel the car sliding out of control. Spinning. Instinctively he cranked the wheel. It did little good—he was going too fast.

Carnival rides flashed through his mind— the rides you have no control over, where you can only sit and scream until they're over— but this ride was short-lived. The left front wheel caught the loose dirt of the shoulder. That was all it took. The dirt slowed the wheels, but the Jeep kept flying sideways.

The Jeep began rolling!

Philip clutched the wheel with his right hand and threw his left arm over his face. Tree trunks, the steep bank, and the road were all jumbled as his body slammed into the driver's-side window, then was thrown up into the roof. The steering wheel jabbed into his legs as glass sprayed in all directions. He wondered dazedly how many times the vehicle was rolling when suddenly it came to a bone-jarring stop.

He'd hit a tree.

Thank God! He was upside down, but at least he wasn't rolling anymore.

No sooner had Philip thought this than the Jeep shuddered and slid down a bank a dozen or so more feet before it finally came to a complete stop. A few pieces of glass tinkled; some clods of dirt fell from the spinning tires. But other than that there was silence . . . except for a faint crackling and popping.

Philip opened his eyes. He was inside, lying on the roof. A blue light flickered in rhythm with the crackling and popping. It took a moment to register before he realized he hadn't hit a tree—he'd hit a power pole.

He tried to move along the inside of the roof, but the shifting of his weight caused the car to creak forward. He looked out the windshield—and froze. A drop-off loomed directly ahead—seventy-five feet of sheer nothing.

Fear rose within him, but he fought it back. He moved again, more cautiously, and again the Jeep started to tip. He stopped. Now he understood. The car was on its top, balancing on a rock or ledge or something. He was safe, but just barely. One wrong move, and he'd send the whole thing plummeting off the cliff.

9

Scott heard the squealing tires and the sickening sound of crunching metal. He knew there'd been an accident just outside the store, but he didn't care. How could he? His best friend had been brutally murdered. *He* had been brutally murdered. With that type of tragedy, how could he pay attention to bothersome things like reality?

Still, he heard customers shouting to one

another and rushing outside, so he figured he'd better join them. Reluctantly he snapped off the laptop, rose, and headed for the front door.

He hadn't felt this bad since his father had died.

～

Becka and Ryan bounced down the driveway in the Mustang, heading as fast as they could toward the main road. Ryan threw the car into a hard right, and they slid onto the asphalt. As he accelerated he shouted, "Where did that thing come from? It just exploded in front of us. One minute it was dark, the next minute brighter than daylight."

"Remember what Z said about them popping in and out of another dimension?"

Ryan glanced at her. "You're thinking the spiritual world again?"

Becka looked straight ahead, hoping she was wrong—fearing she was right.

They rounded the bend in the road. Up ahead was the General Store. A handful of people were rushing out, running across the road.

"There's Scotty!" Becka pointed to the front porch of the store, where her brother slouched against the stair railing, his hands in his pockets. Ryan turned the Mustang into the parking lot and skidded to a stop in front of him.

"Where're they going? What happened?" Ryan shouted out the window.

Scott motioned across the road. "Some sort of accident."

Ryan spun around to look, but Becka stared at Scott. Something was wrong with her brother. "You OK?" she called.

He shrugged.

"Scotty, what's wrong?"

"Don't worry about it."

Before Becka could pry any further, they heard the owner running back toward the store. He was red faced and puffing. "Got to call 911!" he cried. "Some kid flipped his car."

Becka froze. Ryan was already opening his door. "What kind of car?"

"Jeep. The whole thing's balancing on a ledge—could go any second."

Becka leaped out of the car and joined Ryan. They started across the road. She glanced over her shoulder and saw Scott still looking lost. "It's Philip!" she shouted.

He did not move.

"Will you come on?! It's Philip!"

She turned and continued to the other side. When they arrived, they saw what the store owner had described. The Jeep had smashed into a power pole, which had stopped it from flipping over the edge. The car had slid down the soft bank on its top a dozen or so feet until it came to rest on a narrow outcropping of rock. There it balanced precariously, teetering on the edge of the drop-off. The entire scene was bathed in the eerie blue-and-white sparks of a power line that snapped and crackled on the roadway.

"Oh, man . . . ," Ryan whispered. Becka shook her head in stunned silence. They moved past the three or four spectators who were keeping their distance from the dancing cable.

"Philip?" Ryan called. "Philip, can you hear me?"

A faint voice answered from inside the Jeep. "Ryan, is that you?" But even as he spoke, the car shifted forward.

"Don't move!" Becka cried.

Ryan carefully negotiated past the sparking wire. Becka followed gingerly.

"Be careful!" an older woman shouted. "Better wait for the EMS." The others agreed.

But Ryan knew they couldn't wait. Not only was there Philip to worry about, there was Krissi. They moved to the edge of the road. A gentle slope of dirt and gravel led ten or fifteen feet farther to the outcropping of rock where the Jeep was balanced. Just past that was the cliff—and a whole lot of darkness.

Ryan called out, "Looks like you're playing teeter-totter on this here cliff."

"I figured it was something like that,"

Philip shouted. "Listen, I've got to get out of here. I've got to help Krissi."

"One catastrophe at a time, ol' buddy."

"You don't understand." Again the car shifted.

"Philip!" Becka warned.

"Let's see if we can take care of you first," Ryan suggested.

"We've got to hurry, we've got to—" Again the car shifted.

"Philip!"

Philip quit talking and remained still.

Ryan motioned down to the outcropping of granite the Jeep balanced on. There were two, maybe three, extra feet of rock on the right side of the car. Plenty of room for a person to get a foothold and reach out to help Philip.

Becka followed his gaze, then turned on him. "Are you crazy?"

Again the car shifted.

Ryan looked at her. There was her answer. Even if they decided to wait for an EMS, it was doubtful the Jeep would. Already they could hear tiny rocks and bits of granite crumbling and slipping out from under the car. They had to act. Now.

Without another word, Ryan turned and began sliding down the soft slope toward the outcropping of rock. Becka started to follow until he turned to look up at her and demanded, "Where do you think you're going?"

"Same place you are."

He looked at her, trying by sheer intimidation to force her back up the slope. It didn't work.

"Guys?" Philip called. "The side window's popped out. Maybe I can crawl over to it and—"

Again the Jeep tilted forward, only this time it slid an inch or two.

The spectators gasped.

"Philip!" Becka cried.

"I wouldn't do that if I were you," Ryan suggested. He turned to give Becka one last look. She motioned him forward, making it clear that if he didn't take the lead, she would. Reluctantly he turned and continued down the slope. The dirt and gravel slid with them, covering their shoes as they made their way down to the granite outcropping.

Since Ryan had the lead, he was the one to step onto the rock and stoop to look inside at Philip. He grinned. "Hey, bud, got anything for a black eye?"

"Oh, man," Philip groaned. "I didn't mean to do that. I don't know what came over me."

"That's OK. Just don't go getting yourself killed till I get a chance to even the score."

Becka sighed. She hated "machoese." But

having a brother, she knew that type of talk was part of the male routine. Either that or one too many Schwarzenegger movies. She could never tell which.

She went to join Ryan. There wasn't enough room for two on the rock, so she dug in and planted herself in the soft dirt beside him. She also grabbed on to a good, solid bush just to be safe.

"Hey, Beck," Philip called from inside, "how's everything going?"

"Could be better."

"I hear you." He shifted, and more rocks slipped from underneath the Jeep. "Any ideas what to do?"

"You can't make it over to this passenger window?" Ryan asked.

"Not without everything giving way."

"What if I were to reach in and grab you? What if I grab you, you hang on, and I pull you through the window?"

"You mean while the Jeep's falling?" Philip tried to laugh, but it came out more like a semihysterical giggle. More rocks slid away.

"I don't see any other way." Ryan turned to Becka for confirmation. Her mind was churning a thousand miles an hour, looking for an alternative plan, but he was right. The Jeep's granite perch looked as though it would give way at any moment. There was no other plan.

"And if your hands slip?" Philip asked.

"I guess you'll just have to trust me. Time to have a little faith, ol' buddy."

"This isn't another one of your sermons, is it?"

Ryan grinned. "Could be."

"Could be I should just stay put." Philip coughed and the Jeep creaked precariously. "Then again . . ." He swallowed hard and gave a recap. "OK, let me get this straight. I leap across the cab and grab your hand."

"Check."

"That movement sends the Jeep over the cliff."

"Probably."

"But you hang on and pull me through the window as it's falling."

"You got it."

There was a long pause. Ryan and Becka exchanged glances. It was risky, to say the least. But what else could they do?

Finally, Philip answered. "OK."

"All right." Ryan repositioned his feet on the granite for the best stance.

Becka reached out and grabbed Ryan's belt with her free hand, clinging to the bush with the other.

"Beck?"

"Yeah, Philip?"

"Would you, uh . . . I mean . . . would you mind like saying a little prayer?"

Becka was surprised. Then nervous. The last thing in the world she liked to do was to pray out loud. Especially in front of friends. She glanced to the handful of people up on the road. Or in front of crowds.

Still, this was no time for cowardice.

"Sure, Phil," she said, her voice coming out a little hoarse.

More rocks gave way.

"Could you do it, like, soon?"

Becka didn't close her eyes. She looked straight ahead and concentrated on the dirt in front of her. "Dear Lord." She cleared her throat. "Lord, we just ask that you help us do this right. Give Ryan the strength to hang on, and Philip . . . give him the faith to let go and jump. In your name, Jesus . . . Amen."

Ryan muttered a quiet "Amen." Though she wasn't sure, Becka thought she heard one come from Philip, too.

"Well." Philip took a deep breath. "You guys ready?"

Ryan tested his footing one last time and reached his hand into the window. "Let's do it."

"You sure you've forgiven me about that black eye?" Philip said, unable to resist one last chuckle. "Because if you haven't, maybe we should—"

Without further warning, the last of the loose granite slipped away. The Jeep started to slide.

"Philip!" Becka cried.

"Jump!" Ryan shouted. "Jump!"

Philip froze.

"What are you waiting for? Jump!"

The Jeep was sliding away. Without thinking, Ryan lunged into the window.

"Ryan!" Becka screamed as the car's motion pulled him from her grasp. She leaped toward him, grabbing with both hands. She caught his legs and hit the ground. She would not let go. She hung on, pulling him back out of the window as the Jeep continued to slide. She could hear him cry out as the door scraped across his stomach, then banged its way up his ribs, but she hung on until he emerged.

He wasn't alone.

Ryan had grabbed Philip and was hanging on as stubbornly as Becka. His hands were locked on to Philip's wrists in a death grip.

The Jeep continued sliding.

Becka was pulled across the rocky ledge. She still held on to Ryan, who still held on to Philip. Now it was Philip's turn to scream as his upper body scraped through the open window—but his legs still weren't free, and the force of the Jeep's descent pulled all three along the granite toward the precipice.

Becka tried to dig in her feet, her knees, her elbows, anything to slow them down. Ryan did likewise until Philip managed to kick his way out through the window, and he was free—just as the Jeep reached the edge and slipped over, doing a graceful one-and-a-half gainer seventy-five feet into oblivion.

But the trio was still moving. Their momentum on loose stones and gravel made it impossible to stop. All three dug in—flesh and bone against gravel and rock—and cried out in pain. They slowed, then, finally, mercifully, came to a stop. They lay there, bleeding and panting, gasping for air, white billows of breath hovering over their heads. Below, they heard the Jeep explode as it hit bottom.

The noise had barely faded before they heard another sound. One that was much more chilling. A scream. It was distant. Deep in the woods, across the road. And there was no doubt who it was.

They stumbled to their feet. There were plenty of bruises and cuts and scrapes to go around, but there was no time to whine about them.

Another scream.

They scampered up the soft slope to the road, Philip in the lead, Becka and Ryan on his heels.

10

The three ran for all they were worth, crossing the road and starting up a steep, winding driveway. The driveway snaked this way and that for two or three hundred yards. At last they rounded the final turn—and came to a sudden halt.

There was a house in front of them. Well, the skeleton of a house. It was a big, three-story job that was in the process of being built by somebody with lots of bucks. The beams and floors were in, but the walls were only framed, so they could still see through them.

But it wasn't the house that had brought them up short. It was the giant craft hovering fifty feet above them. Philip, Rebecca, and Ryan stood there, staring in disbelief. It was huge. At least the size of a football field. Round, silvery gray with tiny red, green, and yellow lights flashing along the outside. It seemed to hang motionless and absolutely silent.

Ryan was the first to find his voice. "Do you think it's real?"

"What do you mean, 'real'?" Philip asked.

"I mean, is it material or is it . . ." His voice dropped off.

"Or is it what?" Philip demanded.

Becka answered, "Spiritual."

Philip looked at her. "You think all this stuff is spiritual?"

Becka continued watching the craft as Ryan explained, "Krissi's automatic writing, her bizarre behavior, her channeling that so-called alien, that's all basic occult junk."

Becka continued, "Remember the demon who pretended to be an angel?" Becka said. "How he kept speaking through Julie and telling you how cool all this was supposed to be?"

Philip nodded, his mind clicking as he put the pieces together. He remembered all too well the demonic showdown up at the Hawthorne mansion just a few weeks before. That had been his and Krissi's first experience with the supernatural—and Krissi's first episode of automatic handwriting. His memories of the demon disguised as an angel were equally clear. It had spoken through Julie, telling them how blessed they were to be chosen for this encounter. Philip might not understand it all, but he was painfully clear on one point: He definitely was not feeling blessed.

He took a deep breath to steady himself. "Well, demon or not, Krissi needs our help." He started toward the house.

Ryan caught his arm. "Philip, if this stuff isn't physical, you can't fight it physically."

"What do you mean?"

"You can't do it with muscle or with that fancy brain of yours. You've got to fight the spiritual with the spiritual. You've got to fight it with faith."

"No sweat," Philip said, forcing a smile. "Besides, I have you two along, right?"

There was another scream. Philip spun around and looked up to see a light shoot from the bottom of the craft. It struck something he couldn't see up on the top floor of the house. There was another scream. Just as desperate, but more hopeless. Philip bolted for the house.

"Philip, wait up!"

He didn't. He couldn't. In fact, he picked up his pace. If Ryan and Becka wanted to help, great. If not, he'd have to do it on his own. He knew all about faith. He'd had it back at the Jeep when he lunged for Ryan's hand, when he wouldn't let go. He'd had faith in Ryan; now he'd have to have faith in himself.

He arrived at the house and stepped though the front framed wall. The dim outline of steps was directly ahead of him. He took them two at a time. There was another scream, followed by pathetic whimpering. His heart pounded harder. She was above him, up on the third level, where the light was shining.

"Hang on, Krissi. Hang on!"

He reached the second floor, then found the next set of stairs. They were a little trickier to climb, since the steps hadn't been nailed down. A few slipped and fell, but he took little notice as he scrambled up to the third and final floor.

When he emerged, he was blinded by the

light. But it wasn't shining on him. The beam was directed some thirty feet away, blasting down on a makeshift table—a sheet of plywood stretched between two sawhorses. Six, maybe seven, little creatures huddled around the table. Creatures exactly like the one that had appeared in the cabin doorway. And they were all staring and examining . . .

"Krissi!" Philip cried.

She tried to move, to turn and look at him, but something held her down. There were no ropes, no straps. Somehow the light itself held her in place.

He started toward her. Moving across the floor was dangerous since there were only a few loose sheets of plywood laid on the bare joists. But Philip never slowed. He wasn't sure what the creatures were, but they looked small enough for him to take out two or three at a time if he had to. From the way they refused to step aside, it looked as though he might have to.

He was a dozen feet away when one of them raised its hand. A blow struck Philip in the chest. It was as powerful as a karate kick. He staggered back into a wall brace and leaned there a moment, trying to catch his breath.

Ignoring him, the creatures kept their attention on Krissi.

"No!" Krissi screamed. "No, please . . ."

That was all it took. Philip lunged forward, racing toward them.

The first creature looked up and again raised its hand.

This time the blow felt like a Mack truck smashing into him, but instead of throwing Philip into the wall, it lifted and hurled him against a beam in the ceiling. He gasped as the air rushed from his lungs. He tried to move, but something kept pushing him up against the beam. No one held him, nothing touched him—but some invisible force kept pressing his chest, refusing to let him down.

He looked desperately at Krissi. She was deathly pale in the white light. She twisted and screamed as the creatures poked and prodded with various silvery instruments. Her eyes were crazed with fear.

She spotted Philip. "Help me!" she screamed. "Make them stop!"

Using every ounce of his strength, Philip tried to move, but he couldn't. Then, out of the corner of his eye, he spotted Ryan and Becka at the top of the stairs. Becka looked like she was trembling. It could have been from the cold, but Philip didn't think so.

They stood a moment, checking out the situation. Philip wanted to shout at them to hurry, to *do* something—but he couldn't breathe well enough to whisper, let alone shout. Then he saw Becka take a deep breath, and something began to settle over her. He couldn't put his finger on what it was, but . . . well, it was a type of boldness. It wasn't something she worked up. There just seemed to be a power that came over her, out of the blue . . . naturally, quietly. Philip knew Becka hadn't wanted another confrontation like this, but when she took a step forward, he saw a determination—a confidence—filling her face.

She spoke, her voice full of quiet authority. "In the name of Jesus Christ, I command you to stop this!"

The creatures spun around, startled.

Becka didn't flinch.

The creatures pulled back a few feet, opening up the circle around the table and Krissi.

Philip watched as Ryan stepped forward. "You heard her." His voice, too, was calm, filled with confidence. "By the power and authority of Jesus Christ of Nazareth, we command you to leave her alone!"

The light beaming down on the table began to dim and sputter. At the same time, Philip could feel the pressure against his body start to decrease.

"Now!" Becka demanded. "We order you to release her now."

Immediately the light vanished. So did the hold on Philip. He plummeted to the floor and landed with a thud. For a moment he lay there dazed, but his vision came into focus and he turned to watch Becka and Ryan.

Becka took another step toward the creatures. "Who are you?"

No answer. Just lots of nervous looks and fidgeting.

"Answer me," she said. "I demand for you to show us who you are."

Philip was impressed. He had never seen Rebecca talk or act with such strength and authority. Whatever it was, it had made her completely different than the wilting wallflower he normally saw at school.

Not only was he impressed. So were the creatures.

They were terrified.

"Now!" Becka demanded. "Reveal yourselves now!"

At first, Philip thought his eyes were playing tricks on him, but the gray, triangular heads were no longer gray and triangular. In fact, the creatures' entire bodies were changing, morphing into small, bizarre animal-like things. Some resembled grotesque gargoyles; others, monkey-faced trolls with sharp, gnashing fangs; still others, leather-winged gremlins. Philip recognized them immediately. He'd seen those kinds of things only once before. Back at the mansion, when Becka, Scott, and Ryan had battled demons.

Ryan stepped forward shaking his head. "You guys never give up, do you?"

"Ryan . . . ," Becka warned.

Ryan nodded, then turned back to the creatures. "So what will it be, boys? Feel like being cast into the lake of fire?" He started toward them.

"Ryan . . ."

"Or maybe just a trip into a local herd of swine?" He'd barely gotten the words out when his foot came down on the far edge of the loose sheet of plywood. The sheet dipped, leaving nothing but space under Ryan's feet.

Ryan cried out, clawing at the air frantically, trying to keep his balance. Becka tried to grab his arm, but the other edge of the sheet shot up, catching her in the jaw. Her head snapped back, and she fell to the floor as Ryan dropped through the opening and out of sight. Philip heard his cry, then the sickening thud of his body hitting the second-story floor. Then nothing at all.

"Ryan?" he called. "Are you OK?"

No answer.

He rose and hobbled to the edge of the plywood, where he peered down into the darkness. He couldn't see a thing. "Ry?"

"My ankle . . . ," came the faint reply. "I think it's broken."

Before he could respond, Philip heard faint movement beside him. He turned to see Becka stirring.

"Beck, you all right?"

Before she could answer, Philip heard another sound. Little feet. And claws and nails and talons. Scurrying across plywood.

He spun around.

The creatures were coming directly at them! He struggled to his feet. "Becka, look out!"

She was too dazed to move, but she didn't have to worry. The creatures weren't interested in Becka. They were coming at him!

He stepped back, fighting the panic that screamed in his head. He forced all his logic, all his intellect, to the fore. It was OK. He'd seen and heard everything Ryan and Becka had done. Their faith, the power in the way they spoke. He could do that.

He glanced over at Krissi, who now lay motionless.

He had to do it.

Grim resolve filled him again as he looked again at the creatures approaching him. He cleared his throat and, in his most commanding voice, shouted, "I, Philip Andrews, command you—"

"No . . . ," Becka mumbled, shaking her head.

"It's OK," he answered. "I know what I'm doing." Directing his attention back to the creatures, he shouted, "I command you to stop!"

But they didn't. They were a dozen feet away and closing in fast.

"Stop, I said. I command you to stop!"

They gave no response except for a faint twittering—which sounded suspiciously like laughter.

"Philip," Becka muttered. "You can't—you don't have the authority."

"Stay back!" Philip shouted at them. "I command it!"

Nothing worked. They surrounded him, snapping and clawing at his feet. He tried a different tact. "In the name of Jesus Christ, I command—"

But he never finished. The first one leaped onto his leg. Another followed. He tried to kick them off, but their claws dug deep through his pants and into his calves.

"Augh!" he screamed.

Other creatures joined in, scurrying up his legs and grabbing hold of his waist.

"Beck!" he screamed, fighting and trying to slap them off. "Help me!"

Becka tried to sit up but couldn't. "Stop . . . ,"

she choked. But it was unclear whether she was speaking to the creatures or to Philip.

"Beck!"

The frenzied mob had reached his chest, scurrying around and around, pulling themselves onto his shoulders, lashing at his face. Philip staggered. Their paws and talons blocked his vision. He tripped once, twice, then fell to the floor. They swarmed over him relentlessly, tearing at him.

"Help me! Somebody!"

Then another voice spoke out. "In the power and authority of Jesus Christ, I command you to stop!"

The creatures froze.

"Now!"

In a flash, they leaped off Philip and raced for the shadows.

At first Philip didn't recognize the voice, but as he rose to his knees and looked toward the steps, he saw Becka's little brother, Scott.

"Scotty . . ." Becka struggled to sit up.

He rushed over to her. "Are you OK?"

She nodded, rubbing her head. "What about you?"

He shrugged. "I—I guess I got a little carried away with that game thing."

"A little?! But you're OK?"

He nodded. "It's not every day you get

trashed by a ghoul of the fifteenth degree, but I'm all right now."

A groan from below interrupted them.

Concern flooded Becka's face. "Ryan! He fell. . . ." She moved to look over the edge. "Ryan? Can you hear me?"

"I'm OK . . . ," came the faint answer.

"Thank heaven."

"We'll be down in a second," Scott called, keeping a careful eye on the moving shadows around them. "We've got a little cleaning up to do here first." Turning to Philip he asked, "You all right?"

Philip nodded, gingerly feeling the scratches on his face.

"Can you get down there and help Ryan out?"

"Sure," he said, then motioned over his shoulder. "But what about those—"

He was interrupted by a choking, gasping sound. He turned—and went ice-cold. It was the most frightening sight he had ever witnessed.

The creatures were racing toward Krissi, who was still on the table. They leaped into the air and dematerialized into clouds of misty vapor . . . a vapor that rushed into Krissi's gasping mouth. One cloud after another after another was pulled in with each ragged breath she took.

"Stop it!" Scott ordered, but he was too late. The last one had already entered her.

Krissi began to shake. Her whole body vibrated on the table. She struggled to turn toward them, her face filled with fear.

Becka rose unsteadily. With Scott's help she moved toward her friend. Philip followed. As they approached, Krissi tried to say something, but no sound came.

"Krissi?" Philip asked cautiously.

He thought she shook her head, but her trembling was so great he couldn't really tell.

Becka and Scott came to a stop a few feet in front of her. Philip knew Krissi wanted— *needed*—to be held, so he continued past them toward the table.

"Wait a sec," Scott said, reaching out and touching his arm. "It's not over yet."

Philip hesitated.

"Krissi?" Becka asked.

The girl's head rotated toward her.

"Do you want those things to leave?"

Anger shot through Philip. "Of course she does! What sort of stupid question is that?"

Becka ignored him and continued looking directly at Krissi. "It has to be your decision, Krissi. Do you want those things to leave?"

Krissi nodded vigorously.

Becka and Scott exchanged glances, then Becka stepped up to the table. She reached out her hand and laid it on Krissi's trembling shoulders. Her words were quiet and simple, but full of a confident faith. "In the name of Jesus Christ of Nazareth . . . go."

Krissi's body stiffened. Her head shot back and she let out a violent scream. It seemed to last forever as it echoed through the woods, bouncing back and forth against the trees.

And then she collapsed.

Philip moved in to hold her, and this time Becka and Scott did not stop him. He scooped her body into his arms. It was limp. Whatever had been inside of her was gone. It was over. He buried his face in her hair and fought back the tears.

She stirred against him, and a moment later she was wrapping her arms around his neck. "Oh, Philip," she sobbed. "Philip, it was so awful!"

"It's OK," he soothed in a choked voice. "It's OK. You're safe now."

She clung to him even more tightly. Philip looked over her head at Scott and Becka. He could tell they were beat, but they were smiling. He glanced up to the sky. The hovering craft was gone. So were the lights. Everything was back to normal. He buried his face back in Krissi's hair and hugged her fiercely, overwhelmed by love for her—and gratitude that he had her back.

11

The drive home
was long and cramped. Five bruised and bat-
tered bodies squeezed together in a Mustang
did not make for the most comfortable ride.
Of course, the General Store owner had
called up the local doctor and had him
check them all out. One of the neighbors
even offered to let the group spend the

night, but no one was too seriously injured and everyone was anxious to get home. So . . .

Ryan was in no shape to drive. Something about a cracked rib, a sprained wrist, and a torn ankle ligament made that a little impossible. Philip thought he should stay in the back with Krissi, so that left either Becka or Scott to drive. And since Scott was a couple of years shy of a driver's license, that left Becka.

The Highway Patrol had been called about the Jeep, and Philip had to sign a bunch of papers promising that he and his dad would be back up tomorrow or the next day (something Philip wasn't too thrilled about). But for now they were all heading home.

The episode had been the roughest on Krissi. Not only physically, but emotionally. No one was certain what all she had been through. She didn't want to talk about it, and no one wanted to ask. Not for now. It wouldn't have mattered even if they did. As soon as she hit the backseat and Philip wrapped his arm around her, she dropped off into a deep, sound sleep.

"Will she be OK?" Philip asked.

No one spoke.

"Hello?" he tried again.

Finally Ryan answered from the front seat. "I'm afraid it's not completely over."

"What do you mean?"

Ryan and Becka traded looks. It was her turn to speak. "There's an empty space inside Krissi right now, where this Xandrak guy and his jerks were hanging out."

"You mean the demons?" Philip asked.

Becka nodded. "Unless that space gets filled with something or someone . . ." She hesitated. How could she say this diplomatically?

Scott didn't even try. "Then the demons will come back and bring in even more of their buddies."

~

Philip stared at them in disbelief. "You're kidding. Tell me you're kidding."

Scott shook his head. "It's in the Bible."

Philip sighed heavily. He didn't like that answer. Not one bit. "And by 'someone,' you're talking about Jesus, right?"

"That's right," Ryan answered.

Philip took another breath and slowly let it out. "I tell you, I thought I knew about being a Christian, but there's a lot more to this religious stuff than just showing up at church or asking God for junk."

Ryan nodded. "It's a war. People are fighting for their souls. We're all in it, and we all need help. None of us can do it alone."

"I found that out in a hurry," Philip said, tenderly touching the scratches on his neck and face. "It's been a long time since I've been clobbered like that." A moment passed as he remembered Becka's shining faith—and his own failed efforts. Then he shrugged. "Maybe I'll give religion another fling."

"It's gotta be more than a fling," Ryan said. "Christianity's a way of life, Phil. It's loving God and letting him be your boss. That's what *Lord* means. Christ has to be your boss."

"But other Christians don't do that. They're messing up all the time. Like my mom splitting and leaving me and Dad behind. Talk about a hypocrite."

"We're all hypocrites," Scott said quietly.

Philip turned to him, surprised.

"Think about it. I just wasted the last couple of weeks of my life doing something I knew I wasn't supposed to do."

"And?"

"And it nearly wiped me out. But the cool thing is, when I realized I was wrong, I asked God to forgive me. And he did. I blew it— and I'm forgiven. I mean, if you're really sorry and ask, he'll forgive you of anything. That's the whole point."

Philip glanced about the car. He had a million more questions, but he was too tired to ask. Besides, these guys probably didn't have all the answers. Maybe no one did. Maybe that's where faith came in. The same faith that had saved his life. And Krissi's.

He looked down at her. When she woke, they would talk. He would explain all that had happened, all that he had learned. And maybe, just maybe, the two of them would look deeper into Jesus Christ.

He hoped she'd agree. He leaned back and closed his eyes. He sincerely hoped so.

~

Three days passed before Becka checked the computer for any messages from Z. And when she did a cold, hard knot formed in her stomach:

Rebecca, Scott: I received an urgent message on the Internet. A young girl in Louisiana is in trouble. She's deeply involved in voodoo and desperately needs your help. You will soon receive airline tickets by mail. Do not be afraid. Your training is complete. Go in His authority. Z

Author's Note

As I developed this series, I had two equal and opposing concerns. First, I didn't want the reader to be too frightened of the devil. Compared to Jesus Christ, Satan is a wimp. The two aren't even in the same league. Although the supernatural evil in these books is based on a certain amount of fact, it's important to understand the awesome protection Jesus Christ offers to all who have committed their lives to him.

This brings me to my second and somewhat opposing concern: Although the powers of darkness are nothing compared to the power of Jesus Christ and the authority he has given his followers, spiritual warfare is not something we casually stroll into. The situations in these novels are extreme to create suspense and drama. But if you should find yourself involved in something even vaguely similar, don't confront it alone. Find an older, more mature Christian (such as a parent, pastor, or youth leader) to talk to. Let them check the situation out to see what is happening, and ask them to help you deal with it.

Yes, we have the victory through Christ, but we should never send in inexperienced soldiers to fight the battle.

Oh, and one final note. When this series was conceived, there were really no bad guys on the Internet. Unfortunately that has changed. Today there are plenty of people out there trying to draw young folks in to dangerous situations through it. Although the characters in this series trust Z, if you should run into a similar situation, be smart. Anyone can *sound* kind and understanding, but their intentions may be entirely different. All that to say, don't take candy from strangers you see . . . or trust those you don't.

Bill

ENDNOTES

Chapter 1
Information on UFOs taken from Dr. Hugh Ross, *ETs and UFOs* (Pasadena, Calif.: Reason to Believe, 1990), audiocassette.

Chapter 4
Information on role-playing games and the quote from Gary Gygax (p. 50), the creator of Dungeons & Dragons, taken from Joan Hake Robie, *The Truth about Dungeons & Dragons* (Lancaster, Pa.: Starburst, Inc., 1991), 11, 49, 57, 59.

Chapter 5
Information on UFOs taken from Dr. Hugh Ross, *ETs and UFOs* (Pasadena, Calif.: Reason to Believe, 1990), audiocassette.

Quote from Dr. Jacques Valle (p. 70) taken from Michael Lindemann, *UFOs & the Alien Presence: Six Viewpoints* (Santa Barbara, Calif.: The 2020 Group, 1991), 85. Emphasis on demons added.

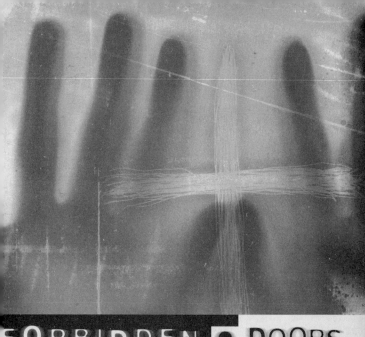

FORBIDDEN ● DOORS

Want to learn more?

Visit Forbiddendoors.com on-line for
special features like:

- a really cool movie
- post your own reviews
- info on each story and its
  characters
- and much more!

Plus—Bill Myers answers your questions!
E-mail your questions to the author. Some
will get posted—all will be answered by
Bill Myers.

WheRe
AdvEnture
beGins
with
a BoOk!

LoG oN @
Cool2Read.com